"If you are upset, I want you to tell me."

Verna nodded slowly. "All right. Then I will say it. When you marched out of the house, I felt terrible. I didn't like that feeling of you just turning your back."

Adam had made her feel that way by simply going outside? Women were complex creatures, weren't they? Had she preferred him to stand inside and struggle to breathe?

"Okay," Adam said carefully. "I can see that. I had thought our conversation was over."

She'd been heading upstairs to put Amanda Rebecca back to bed. Had she wanted him to wait for her to come back down?

"I would say our conversation isn't over until we feel better," she said.

That might make for some long conversations.

"Okay," he said. "I'm sorry that I upset you, too."

A smile touched the corners of her lips. "*Danke*, Adam. I want us to be happy."

"Me, too." Desperately. Deeply. He longed for it, but he was starting to worry it wouldn't be so easy.

Patricia Johns is a *Publishers Weekly* bestselling author who writes from Alberta, Canada, where she lives with her husband and son. She writes Amish romances that will leave you yearning for a simpler life. You can find her at patriciajohns.com and on social media, where she loves to connect with her readers. Drop by her website and you might find your next read!

Books by Patricia Johns

Love Inspired

Amish Country Matches

The Amish Matchmaking Dilemma
Their Amish Secret
The Amish Marriage Arrangement
An Amish Mother for His Child

Redemption's Amish Legacies

The Nanny's Amish Family
A Precious Christmas Gift
Wife on His Doorstep
Snowbound with the Amish Bachelor
Blended Amish Blessings
The Amish Matchmaker's Choice

Visit the Author Profile page at LoveInspired.com for more titles.

An Amish Mother for His Child

Patricia Johns

LOVE INSPIRED
INSPIRATIONAL ROMANCE

LOVE INSPIRED®
INSPIRATIONAL ROMANCE

Recycling programs for this product may not exist in your area.

ISBN-13: 978-1-335-59852-3

An Amish Mother for His Child

Copyright © 2023 by Patricia Johns

For questions and comments about the quality of this book, please contact us at CustomerService@Harlequin.com.

Love Inspired
22 Adelaide St. West, 41st Floor
Toronto, Ontario M5H 4E3, Canada
www.LoveInspired.com

Printed in U.S.A.

Husbands, love your wives,
even as Christ also loved the church.
—*Ephesians* 5:25

To my husband. You're still the only one for me.
I love you!

Chapter One

Snow swirled down from a heavy, gray sky. It spun past the windowpanes and made the January early afternoon feel more like dusk. Kerosene lamps hissed quietly, illuminating Bishop Zedechiah and Trudy Glick's sitting room in their soft glow. Verna Kauffman shivered despite the woolen cardigan she wore over her blue cape dress. Maybe it was nerves.

The furniture had all been moved aside to make room for the few guests—Verna's parents, her grandfather, her great-grandmother who sat to the side in a rocking chair, her sister and her family. And, of course, the community matchmaker, Adel Knussli, was there, too, with her husband, Jacob, at her side and their toddler son on her hip. She was responsible for setting up this marriage, after all. It

was through Adel's connections that Verna
had found her soon-to-be husband. Adam
Lantz was from Oregon, but he seemed kind
and decent, and he was a widowed father in
need of a mother for his little girl. And Verna
was a woman of thirty who'd never managed
a match before this one.

This was Verna's chance, and she sucked
in a steadying breath as the bishop's sono-
rous words passed over her. He was preaching about the duties of marriage—taking care
of each other, loving each other, respecting
each other and raising the children in the right
paths. She tried to listen, but her heart was
pounding so hard that she couldn't follow it.
She glanced over at Adam. He was looking
down at his polished boots, a solemn expression on his face. He was taller than her, with
curling blond hair that refused to keep to the
Amish haircut. His jaw was strong, and he
already had a red-gold married beard, since
he'd been married before. There was no needing to guess what marriage would look like
on him. Adam seemed to feel her gaze because his eyes flickered in her direction, and
he gave her a small smile.

This man—this virtual stranger—was
going to be her husband.

The room was warm—the potbellied stove

pumping heat against her side—but her fingers were still cold. She didn't have time to carefully sew her own blue wedding cape dress. Her *mamm* had helped her to adjust a blue dress she already owned, and to sew a crisp new white apron to go with it. There was no wedding quilt waiting for her bed, either. She'd have to sew her own after the event, in the long, cold months ahead. But here she stood on this most important day, wondering if she'd feel different after those vows were said—if being married had a feeling all its own.

"We have now come to the vows," Bishop Glick said. He was a plump man with kind eyes and a salt-and-pepper, grizzled beard. "These vows are for life. There is no breaking them. There is no going back on them. For the rest of your lives, you will be bound to each other in all situations—husband and wife."

Verna smoothed her hands down the front of her apron.

"Do you, Adam Lantz, vow to be the husband of Verna Kauffman, to protect and provide for her, to honor and cherish her, for all of your days?"

Would he? Now that it came down to the line, would Adam really vow to be hers? She didn't look at him, didn't allow herself so much as a glance. She swallowed, her head starting to buzz.

"*Yah*, I do."

She exhaled, her head feeling light.

"And do you, Verna Kauffman, vow to be the wife of Adam Lantz, to love and support him, to honor and cherish him for all of your days?"

Verna nodded. "*Yah*, I do."

"Then I pronounce the blessing on you of Abraham and Sarah, Isaac and Rebecca, of Jacob and Rachel. You are wed. What Gott has joined, let no man separate."

Verna didn't move, and then she felt Adam's hand brush hers. She looked over and found Adam looking at her hesitantly. They were married.

"Congratulations," Bishop Glick said, leaning forward and giving her a warm smile. Then he shook Adam's hand.

Next there was a hymn, followed by another, and Verna stood there, feeling like she might fall over from the rush of it all. It was done—he'd vowed, she'd vowed... They were married! And when Bishop Glick said the last prayer, Verna turned to see her mother, Hannah, with tears in her eyes. She stood next to Great-Grandmother Sarah's rocking chair, the old woman's hand in hers.

Hannah's hair was iron gray, and she had lines around her eyes and around her mouth. Verna was the youngest child in the family, and she knew that her mother was both relieved and a little nervous about Verna's marriage.

Verna's father was on the other side of the room with Jacob Knussli. He came forward to shake Adam's hand, and Hannah came and gave Verna a tight hug.

"A married woman now," her mother whispered in her ear. "May you be very happy, my dear girl."

She pulled back and tears sparkled in her eyes.

"I will be," Verna said firmly. "I will."

She was determined to be happy. She might hardly know this man, but this was her chance, wasn't it? She now had a family— Adam and Amanda Rebecca, his daughter.

Trudy Glick, the bishop's wife, stood back with the little girl in her arms. Amanda Rebecca was nearly five, and she had big, somber blue eyes and hair pulled back away from her face that was so fair that it was almost white. She was one reason Verna had agreed to this wedding—a tiny little girl who needed a *mamm* of her own so very badly. Amanda Rebecca was why Adam had been looking for a marriage arrangement, too. Adam was a loving father, but he was so formal and needed some help in raising a girl. Well, Verna had longed to be a mother for as long as she could remember, and now there was a little child who would well and truly belong to her.

Trudy put Amanda Rebecca down, and the little girl went over to Adam's side. She stood very still, her hands folded in front of her pink cape dress, a little white cardigan on top to keep her warm.

Adam turned, looked down at his daughter and then over at Verna, and in that moment, Verna felt like a gate had closed—like the three of them were shut inside a circle that belonged to only them. Verna walked closer, and Adam smiled at her.

"Amanda Rebecca," Adam said, his voice low and quiet. "Verna is now your *mamm*. We talked about this, didn't we?"

"Yah," the girl whispered.

"You will need to mind her and do as she says, okay?"

"Okay." The same small whisper.

"She'll show you all the things I can't show you," Adam went on. "She'll show you how to dress, and how to sew and cook, and how to grow up to be a good girl."

"I'm a good girl already," she said softly.

"*Yah*, but you need a *mamm* for so many things. You'll have to call Verna Mamm now."

Amanda Rebecca looked up at Verna, and her chin trembled. Would this child call her Mamm anytime soon? She was small and frail, but she had a spine of steel in her—that was easy to see. She might not be the type to kick up a fuss, but she wasn't going to bend before she was ready, either.

Verna squatted down in front of the child and looked into those big, soulful eyes.

"I'm so happy to be your new *mamm*," she said. "I'll take very good care of both you and your *daet*. We'll be a happy family. I promise."

Amanda Rebecca just looked at her mutely. She didn't seem happy or unhappy, but small and a little stunned. She didn't reach for her father's hand, either—Verna had noticed that for a young child, Amanda Rebecca seemed very self-reliant. Perhaps too self-reliant.

But that was where Verna's job began. She'd have to bond with her little stepdaughter and give her the love and care that only a woman could give. Adam had been right about that—there were some things only a mother could teach. Gott had brought Verna and Adam together for a reason, and the reason that burned in Verna's heart stood before her in a little pink cape dress with blue eyes round with trepidation.

"Are you hungry yet?" Verna asked her.

Amanda Rebecca shook her head.

"Say no, Mamm," Adam prompted her.

"No, I'm not hungry," the girl whispered.

Verna almost smiled at the quick verbal sidestep. She was a smart one—and Verna was rather proud of her already. Verna stood up again and faced her new husband. Adam didn't look as nervous as she felt, but then he'd been married before so this wasn't entirely new for him. For Verna, she'd been dreaming of her wedding day for years…and then she'd given up dreaming, thinking she'd never get her chance. So standing here on the day of her wedding, looking at the man she was now joined to for the rest of her life, she felt a little thrill of fear.

The rest of their lives…and they hardly knew each other. Was this foolhardy? A little late to consider that, though. It was done.

"Well…" Verna wasn't really sure what to say in a moment like this one.

"How does it feel?" Adam asked.

"I don't know yet," she admitted. "You?"

"I think we'll be just fine," he replied seriously.

"The things we promised before…" she said. "We'll keep those promises, won't we?"

He nodded, a smile touching his lips. "*Yah.* Of course, we will. I'll be good to you."

And she knew he would be. That was one thing she felt utterly certain of—Adam Lantz would be good to her. She'd been reassured of that fact by Adel, who'd looked very closely into his history and talked to a bishop and two deacons who knew Adam personally. She'd sat down with him for some extensive interviews, too, and at the end of her digging, Adel had proclaimed him a good man. That meant something—Adel didn't play games when it came to deciding upon someone's character. But all the same, Adel had also given a warning: *He's a good man. He'll fulfill his duties, and you can be certain he'll never lie to you. But he's reserved, and I'm afraid that will seep over into his marriage relationship, as well. That's my concern. I won't sugarcoat it.*

"Verna?"

Verna turned and saw her father a few feet away, and she moved over to accept a hug from him. Behind him, her *mamm* was helping Great-Grandmother to stand up and get steadied on her feet. At 101 years old, Great-Grandmother was doing very well.

"I'm happy for you, Verna," her father said earnestly. "You deserve this."

"*Danke*, Daet," she said. "I'll be a good wife."

"Of course, you will be," he replied. "You're a wonderful cook, a good seamstress, and you've got a heart of gold. Adam is blessed to have gotten you."

Daet always did know how to make her feel better. He patted her shoulder again and then looked over at Adam.

"I don't want to keep you from your husband. But when you have time and Adam is working, you should bring your new daughter and come visit your mother and me. The house will be empty without you." Her father dropped his hand and gave her a nod. Daet didn't show much emotion, so even this much meant his heart was overflowing.

She'd miss living in the same house as her parents, too, she realized in a rush. Very much.

"I have some food waiting in the kitchen," Trudy said, raising her voice to be heard. "If you'd like to come to the table, we'll have a meal. It's not a proper wedding without proper eating, is it?"

Verna looked over at strong, handsome Adam, and she sucked in a wavering breath.

There was no confusion here. This marriage had nothing to do with love and everything to do with meeting their needs. Verna needed a husband, and Adam needed a wife. Besides, they'd discussed the most important issues in Adel's kitchen. And Adam had promised her three things—she could continue teaching her knitting class, she would have her own bedroom until she felt more comfortable and they would make their home here in Redemption with her friends and family. Verna was hoping that Adel's worries would be for naught and they'd grow to love each other over the next few months—that Gott would honor those well-intentioned vows and bestow His love into their marriage.

Besides, Verna had a lot of support here in Redemption as she ventured into this new territory of womanhood. Her parents were here, her grandparents, her friends, cousins and a community that had known her since she was born. She wasn't alone. She'd have their support, advice and guidance as she figured out how to be a wife and mother in short order.

Because a whole new life started right now!

Adam followed Verna toward the kitchen. Amanda Rebecca walked stoically at his side. The place for the bride and groom was clear—they had two special plates and tall goblet glasses to drink from. Everyone else had regular plates and glasses. He moved forward to pull Verna's chair out for her, and she smiled her thanks.

Adam sat down next to his wife at the table... *His wife*. She was a regal-looking woman—tall, slim, calm and with creamy skin that looked soft. He'd never touched her cheek, though, so he wouldn't know. She sat next to him, her back straight and her hands in her lap. And Amanda Rebecca sat almost as regally on the chair on the other side of him, perched on top of a little booster seat to get her high enough at the table to reach her plate.

The others took their seats, too. Verna's parents put her great-grandmother between them, and Verna's mother, Hannah, tenderly tucked a napkin into the top of the old woman's dress. Great-Grandmother Sarah lifted her watery gaze to meet Adam's, and her face crinkled up into a smile. She gave him a silent nod, and he found himself feeling a little choked up. This was his new family.

His own *mamm* had been an Englisher by birth, and that stigma had always clung to their family. His *mamm* hadn't made cabbage rolls like anyone else, and she'd never fully understood Amish humor. She'd spoken Pennsylvania Dutch with an accent, but she'd loved her family well…even though she'd been different—always so different. She didn't hide her emotions like other Amish women. And she wasn't nervous around Englishers, either. Obviously, she knew them better. Her parents sometimes visited, and he'd see his *mamm* laughing with them in a way that Amish adults didn't do with their parents.

Being the son of such a different woman had been hard for Adam in his youth, and it had been important to him that his wife be a proper Amish woman with Amish pedigree—less for people to pick on. And Verna was proper in every way. With Verna, he and his daughter could settle into the comfortable middle of Amish life.

The meal was served, and Verna didn't eat much—just moved the food around the plate with her fork and took a small bite now and again. Adam didn't feel hungry, either. The food smelled wonderful, and he knew he'd be hungry later, but right now he just felt nervous. He ate without thinking, though. He was used to hard physical work—a man didn't pass up a good meal just because he didn't feel like eating it.

"Adam, have a little more noodles," Trudy said, scooping another helping onto his plate.

"Danke," he said, but he wasn't sure he'd be able to eat it all.

He looked over at Verna and caught her eye. Color touched her cheeks, and she dropped her gaze.

His wife.

It had been four years since he'd last been a married man. Four years since he'd lost Rebecca. And four years since he vowed he'd never be a husband again. He wasn't any good at it. But he wasn't very good at raising a daughter alone, either, and after his sister had gone off to Florida to marry an Amish man out there, he'd been left alone with his daughter and a growing certainty that he needed a wife.

Of course, everyone around him thought his worries that he wasn't very good at marriage were silly. They encouraged him to meet some eligible women and start again. *You'll be fine,* they said. *You'll see how much a woman will bring to your home, and you'll be grateful you did it.*

His bishop, however, had stayed ominously silent on the matter. His silence still bothered Adam. If he thought Adam should have just stayed a single widower, he should have said so. That was a bishop's duty, wasn't it? But he hadn't said a word. All he said was that

Adam should do what he thought was best, as if Adam even knew what that was.

But Adam's sister and parents had all been so eager when they saw a crack in his determination to stay single, and they'd immediately contacted Redemption's matchmaker. With his grandfather's connection to this community, he'd suggested it. Besides, they'd heard about some quality single women in Redemption through friends, and Adam wanted to explore those old family connections. Plus, the matchmaker had a very good reputation. There was one woman suggested, but she changed her mind about being ready for a match. He thought it might be a sign, and was ready to give up then, but the machine had been set into motion and Adel had come up with another match—Verna Kauffman. He'd agreed to meet her.

Somehow, Adam ate the meal in front of him. He didn't remember much of it. Trudy, Adel and Verna's mother, Hannah, all made a fuss over Amanda Rebecca and plied her with more pie than meat and vegetables. Normally, Adam insisted upon a nutritious meal first, but he couldn't exactly do that right now, and Amanda Rebecca did seem to be relaxing with a big mouthful of cherry pie, her proper meal pushed to the side.

When the meal was over, the bishop said a prayer to bless their marriage, goodbyes were said and Adam went outside to hitch up the buggy. Jacob Knussli, the matchmaker's husband, went with him, and together they sorted out the straps.

"It's a big day," Jacob said, casting him a smile.

"Yah." Adam wasn't sure what else to say. He didn't know these people very well, although Jacob had been part of helping him find some local work at a large, Englisher dairy farm. He'd never worked a farm like this before. Back home in Oregon, he'd worked the small Amish farm with his brother and part-time at a canning factory.

"Verna's a really wonderful woman," Jacob said. "You've got a good wife, there."

"Danke. Yah, I think so, too."

"If you ever want to come by for a visit, Adel and I would love to have you."

"I appreciate it." Adam tightened the last strap. But a newly married couple visiting the matchmaker again normally meant they needed some help in sorting out a dispute. He wouldn't be needing that.

"Well… Congratulations again," Jacob said with a smile.

Verna must have been watching, because

she came outside then, Amanda Rebecca at her side. She took the little girl's hand and led her across the snowy ground to the buggy. Adam picked up his daughter under her arms and swung her into the buggy first, and then he offered Verna his hand.

"Danke..." Verna said, and she accepted his boost into the buggy. She didn't need his help—that had been pure politeness—but he liked the way her hand had felt in his.

He hopped up into the driver's side of the buggy and leaned forward to see outside. Jacob Knussli and Verna's father, Marvin, stood on the step. They both waved. Marvin looked sober...a little worried even. Were Verna's parents pleased with him for their daughter? He wasn't sure. They were being supportive of Verna's choice—that was all he knew.

Adam settled back into the seat and flicked the reins.

"Off we go home," he said, trying to sound cheery. He looked over at Verna. She was looking out the small, square buggy window at the people disappearing behind them. She turned forward.

Adam was married again, and while he knew he needed everything that Verna would bring to his home, it still felt strange. Adam wasn't at his best as a husband. He tended to disappoint, but hopefully Verna's expectations would be lower. Hopefully, she'd be happy with what marriage gave her, too.

Adam had rented a little property just outside of town. It had a chicken coop that was currently empty, a stable, a three-bedroom house and, under the blanket of snow, a generously large garden, he'd been told. He'd cleaned the house himself and set up the bedrooms—one for each of them. That had been his agreement with Verna—she'd have her own room when they started out. He understood. They were virtual strangers.

He reined in close to the door and Verna got down. Amanda Rebecca looked at Adam questioningly.

"Go with...your *mamm*." The words still felt a little strange coming out of his mouth.

His daughter leaned over and let Verna lift her down to the ground, and the two headed over to the house.

Adam took his time unhitching and getting the horse settled in the warm stable. He wasn't sure what held him back—just nervousness, he figured. Because when he walked into that house today, Verna was going to have expectations of him. And he'd have some of her, too.

After he'd done all he needed to in the stable, he had no more excuses, and he headed across the snowy yard, walked up the steps and opened the side door.

There was no mudroom in this house, and the door opened straight into the kitchen. Verna crouched in front of the woodstove, kindling a fire, and Amanda Rebecca stood in the middle of the kitchen looking mildly confused.

Verna turned when she heard him and cast him a smile. "Just getting a fire started."

"Yah, danke." He took off his coat, even though it wasn't exactly warm inside yet, and he put his hat on a peg on the wall. He crossed over to an oak rolltop desk in the sitting room, opened it and took out a folded piece of paper. Then headed back into the kitchen.

The fire crackled in the stove, and Verna closed the stove door. Then she took off her coat and hung it next to his.

"I…uh… I thought it might be helpful if I wrote a few things down for you," Adam said.

Verna turned. "Oh?"

"Just a few things that I want to make sure go smoothly for Amanda Rebecca," he said. He unfolded the paper and looked down at his own handwriting. "First of all, I want her to eat vegetables every day. She isn't to have her dessert until all her vegetables are eaten. There is no flexibility on that."

He glanced up to see Verna looking at him with her eyes wide. What she was feeling, he had no idea, so he just plunged on.

"Also, I want Amanda Rebecca to be called by her full name at all times. Rebecca is her mother's name, and I think I owe her mother that much. I have other reasons, but suffice it to say, I want her to be called by her full name."

"Okay…" Verna crossed her arms and cocked her head to one side.

"I also want her to memorize one Bible passage a month. She must be able to repeat it to me on the first of the month, so you'll need to help her learn it. The first passage she'll be learning is Ephesians, the sixth chapter, verses one through three."

There was silence from Verna.

"And her bedtime is at seven thirty every night, no exceptions."

Adam folded the page and handed it over. Verna accepted it, looked down at his handwriting and nodded.

"Am I…a nanny?" she asked at last.

"No, you're her new mother," he said. "I

just thought that if I wrote it down, it might be easier for you. That's all."

"Am I to make any decisions for her on my own?" she asked.

"Of course. There will be plenty of things that are in the female domain. I won't interfere," he said.

"Good." Verna pressed her lips together. "Isn't she a little young for memorizing that many verses of scripture at once?"

"I don't think so," he replied. "It's important to know her Bible."

Verna sucked in a long, slow breath. Then she nodded. "All right. You've made yourself clear. Do you have a list like that for you?"

"What do you mean?" he asked with a frown.

"A list of things you expect me to do properly for you?" she said. "We might as well get this out of the way now. Expectations for what I'll serve for breakfast, for example? The way you want your laundry done?"

Was she angry? Adam wasn't sure. She had the list clutched in one hand, and she was eyeing him with an uncomfortably calm look on her face. Almost too calm.

"No, of course not. I'm sure that will all be just fine," he replied.

"All right, then." Her tone was quiet, and

all the warmth from earlier was gone. Okay—
he could tell he'd upset her now.

"I don't mean to offend," Adam said. "We
don't know each other, Verna. This is…dif-
ficult for both of us. I thought that being up-
front and clear about what I was expecting
would be better than having talk after talk
about little things that I want done a certain
way. We said we'd communicate openly."

"We did say that," she said. "I wasn't expecting an itemized list, though."

"Oh." He nodded. "I can take it back." He
reached for the page.

"No, no," she said. "I'll keep it. You're right.
It's best to be clear about what we expect, and
you've been clear. *Danke* for that."

"Do you have any expectations from me?"
he asked.

"That you'll pay the bills, keep food in the
house and be honest with me always," she
said.

Of course, he'd do all of those. He'd provide as best he could, and he'd take pride in
making sure his wife and daughter had all
they needed, and even a little extra.

"I will do all of those things," he said.

"Do you want me to write it down?" she
asked, and there was a small smile on her lips.

"No." He smiled faintly back. "I've got it."

The heat from the stove emanated through the room. Verna turned away from him and bent down to take Amanda Rebecca's coat off. She smiled at his daughter as she stood up and went to hang the little coat next to her own.

And standing there in the kitchen, looking at his coat, Verna's coat and Amanda Rebecca's coat all hung up in a row, it suddenly hit him, right in the heart.

He was well and truly *married*.

Chapter Two

Verna looked down at the list Adam had given her once more. There was no message to her personally, no affectionate sign-off at the bottom—just a numbered list. It stung; she had to admit that she had expected at least a bit of pretending that there was some tenderness between them. They were married, after all. The hope was that softer feelings would grow, wasn't it? She looked up at Adam, but his expression was granite.

Maybe he didn't hope for that. That was a sobering thought. Maybe she was the only one hoping this marriage would warm with time. Adel had warned her.

"The house is your domain, obviously," Adam said. "You will run it as you see fit, and I will be grateful for your efforts."

"Much appreciated," she murmured.

"Except for my bedroom, of course," he said. "We did agree to separate bedrooms to start, so for now, that will be my own space. I don't expect you to clean it, make my bed or otherwise bother with it."

"I don't see how that's possible," she said. "I'll have to wash linen, and I'll have to put away laundry."

"Right..." He cleared his throat. "I suppose all I meant is that if I'm messy or something, I don't want you to feel obliged to clean up after me—not in that room, at least."

"I'm your wife," she said.

What she meant was that he was going to be her problem. He'd also make more messes than in just one room. She'd be cleaning the bathroom, the kitchen, the sitting room. She'd be mopping the floor from muddy boots and cleaning sinks. She'd be doing his laundry, cooking his meals, washing his dishes, raising his daughter—and that one room was supposed to make her burden less? She'd chosen this!

"Amanda Rebecca, could you run upstairs and arrange your toys?" Adam asked.

"Okay..." The girl headed for the stairs, but she glanced over her shoulder with a troubled look on her face. She would know that her father was getting her out of the room. She went up the stairs and disappeared from sight.

"You asked me to be honest." Adam took a step closer and lowered his voice. "Do you want that honesty now?"

"*Yah*. Please."

"I'm not...good at this," he said. "Perhaps you've noticed already. I want to be. I want to be the kind of husband you'll be glad you married. I want to give you financial comfort, a cozy home and the respect that a wife is due. But... I irritated Rebecca a lot. I was messy, I was told. I said all the wrong things."

Did he give her a list, Verna wondered? All the same, her irritation was a sad thing to remember about a late wife.

"And you don't want to irritate me with the state of your bedroom," Verna clarified.

"*Yah!*" Adam's expression relaxed. "I don't want to irritate you with anything. I realize I'm not off to an ideal start here. We've just stepped into the house, and I can tell I've already upset you. I don't mean to. I think that's what you need to know about me. I might step wrong, but it is never intentional."

"I'll remember that," Verna said. "And I can promise you that while I will clean the linens and do your laundry, I will never comment on the state of your bedroom."

"Danke." He smiled gratefully.

An Amish man with a tendency toward mess wasn't unheard of, but he normally had a strong wife with an inclination to clean it behind him.

"Would you like to see the room I put together for you?" Adam asked.

"Yes, please," she said.

A smile touched Adam's lips, and he looked at her with a sudden fondness that made her catch her breath.

"We did our best with your bedroom," he said. "Of course, you'll have your own ideas of what makes for comfort. But I think we did well, my daughter and I."

So they'd worked together on her room—that was a rather sweet thought. The girl appeared on the staircase and came down a few steps, those round eyes fixed on Verna uncertainly.

"Amanda Rebecca," Verna said with a smile. "Do you want to show me my room?"

The girl nodded, and a smile erupted over her face.

"Yah! I'll show you!"

Verna wasn't quite sure why she did it, but somehow, going alone with her own husband upstairs felt a little more intimate than she was ready for, and this little chaperone would do nicely.

Verna held her hand out to the girl, and Amanda Rebecca came down the last of the stairs and slipped one cold little hand into Verna's grasp. Verna put her other hand over the girl's chilled fingers.

"Then we'll warm you up by the stove," Verna said. "I'm going to go through the cupboards and find something warm and tasty I can make for you. Would you like that?"

Amanda Rebecca nodded. "*Yah.* I'd like that. My auntie used to make me hot chocolate."

"If we have cocoa, I'll make some, too," Verna said.

Somehow, offering some nurturing to this little girl seemed easier than offering it to the child's serious, reserved father.

Adam gave an approving nod. "I believe we have some. But only after a sensible piece of bread."

Verna met the girl's gaze and shrugged. If that was the price for hot chocolate, so be it. Then Adam started up the stairs, and Verna and Amanda Rebecca followed him. Funny— in this brand-new marriage, this little girl was the one making this house feel like a home. Some women were nervous about becoming a stepmother, but Verna was thrilled. This child needed love, and that was something that Verna had in abundance.

Adam led the way, and when they emerged onto the second floor, Amanda Rebecca tugged Verna along with her down the hallway.

"This is my room," Amanda Rebecca said.

"Amanda Rebecca," Adam said briskly.

The girl stopped in her tracks.

"Show me in a minute, okay?" Verna whispered. "I really want to see your room, too!"

Adam waited at a bedroom door that was ajar. He pushed it open with a long, low squeak of old hinges, and Verna looked inside at a room that was neat and clean.

Blue curtains were tied back with a sash, revealing the snowy scene outside the window, a few flakes spinning past the glass. A chimney went up one side of the bedroom, making the room comfortably warm. The bed was made with a large, fluffy-looking pile of quilts—three that she could count, all different colors and patterns that were visible at the corner of the bed where they converged. Her hope chest had been delivered and sat in a corner of the room. She'd go through it later and unpack. Her dresses were already hanging in the open closet, and her suitcase sat on the wooden floor next to the bed. On the dresser sat a basket.

Verna went over to the basket and pulled it closer to look inside. There were fresh skeins of yarn in a variety of colors—yellow, pink, blue, black. There didn't seem to be any rhyme or reason, just a wonderful, random collection of yarn of different thicknesses and material. Some obviously wool, some acrylic, some cotton. It brought a smile to her lips.

"I know you like to knit, since you teach that knitting class to the Englisher young people," Adam said. "So I bought some yarn for you. I don't know if it's the right kind or the right colors, but—" He stopped short, and Verna looked back at him. Adam shrugged. "I just chose colors that I liked."

She had an image in her mind of this stern man poring over a yarn bin, and it was endearingly sweet. Besides, she'd have quite a bit of time on her own in the evenings—when her husband had gone to bed and their daughter was already asleep. Those long, lonely evenings would need filling, and this basket of yarn would help with that.

"Danke," she said. And she truly meant it.

"If you don't like the colors, the lady at the craft store said we could exchange them for something you like better," he said. "She thought you might have your own ideas of what you needed."

"No, I like what you chose," she said. "Very much."

She would knit with every single skein he'd bought. Pot holders for herself, and then Amanda Rebecca would need all sorts of items to keep her warm in these winter months: mittens, hats, scarves and little cardigans. She'd be the best-cared-for child in Redemption, and that was a promise she was making to herself. There would be no returning Adam's thoughtful gift.

"You like the colors?" he asked.

"I do. Very much. This will keep me knitting for a while. It was kind of you."

Adam looked relieved then, and he nodded a couple of times. "Good. I'm glad. I did do my best to choose the best of what was there."

"You did a good job," she said.

He nodded again. "Okay, well…"

"The room looks very nice," she added. "I'll be comfortable here."

"Good." Adam cleared his throat. "My room is across the hall from you."

Verna looked past him, but the door across the hallway from her was shut. That was the bedroom that would be messy, and she felt an overwhelming urge to get a look at it. Just how messy could one man be? He'd put together a very neat and tidy space for her…

"Do you want to see *my* room now?" Amanda Rebecca asked.

"*Yah*, I do." Verna smiled down at her. "Let's go see."

Verna let the girl tug her past Adam, and her sleeve brushed across his shirt as she was swept out the door past him.

Adam smelled nice, she realized in that fleeting moment of contact. He smelled like the aftershave he used on his top lip and the tops of his cheeks when he would neaten his beard every morning. And she liked that.

If he wanted lists, she was going to start one of her own: things she liked about her new home and family.

And item number one was the smell of Adam's aftershave.

"This is my room," Amanda Rebecca said, pulling Verna into a small bedroom next to her father's.

Amanda Rebecca seemed to take after her father in her tidiness. Two soiled dresses lay across her floor, and Verna resisted the urge to pick them up. There were toys strewn over the top of her rumpled bed—wooden animals, two faceless dolls, a stuffed elephant and a crocheted Noah's Ark set that had a brown boat and a rather impressive array of animals to go inside. Verna recognized it as the handiwork of her friend Lydia. She bent down and picked up a little crocheted giraffe.

"My *daet* got me this ark from the craft store," Amanda Rebecca said. "It's new."

"It's lovely. I think I know the lady who made it," Verna said.

"Yah?"

"Yah. She's very good with a crochet hook. I'm going to teach you how to knit and crochet, too. Do you want to learn?"

"Yah!"

Verna smiled. "In fact, Amanda Rebecca, I have a class I'm teaching tomorrow, and I can bring you with me. Our very first outing together." Adam cleared his throat behind her, and she turned. "If that's okay with you, Adam."

Did she need permission to take her stepdaughter out?

"There are Englishers there," he said. "And you'll be busy with them."

He didn't fully approve of her teaching this class—she'd known that from the start—but she wasn't giving it up. Adam could have his bedroom mess, and she would have her knitting class. Everyone brought something to a marriage.

"This is a partnership between our Amish community and the Englisher community here in Redemption," Verna said. "The government workers were hoping that the at-risk youth can learn something from us, and they do. These teens are really special, Adam. I actually think I've learned more from them than they have from me."

"I don't see how," he said curtly.

"Because I didn't see them as people before this," she said. "Not like us. I saw them as... heathen, I suppose. But then I got to know them, and I saw that they're really just *kinner* that slipped through the cracks somehow. And not all of them will sort themselves out, but some will! And I'm part of that."

The look on Adam's face told her that he wasn't convinced. This might take more time to explain to him, so she let it go.

"All right. Maybe next time," she said, then turned to Amanda Rebecca. "If your *daet* is home from work, you'll stay with him and have a special evening just you and your father. And if he's still working, then you will come with me, and he will know that you are safe with your new *mamm*. Does that sound fair?"

Adam shuffled his feet, then sighed. "*Yah.* I'll be sure to be home on time."

Good. Because Verna would gladly love and care for both Adam and Amanda Rebecca, but she would not give up her contributions in Redemption.

Adam needed a mother for his daughter—that was clear. But he hadn't fully opened himself to having a proper wife. Well, a woman needed to be needed, and the beautiful thing about life here in Redemption was that a woman could find a place where what she had to offer was just what another person needed most.

Even if that other person was an Englisher teenager at a knitting class.

That evening, Adam sat at the table, watching as Verna and Amanda Rebecca stood over the woodstove with a whisk, stirring a steaming pot of hot cocoa. Their backs were to him, both leaning together as they looked into the pot. Verna's blue wedding dress—she hadn't taken it off yet—contrasted with Amanda Rebecca's little pink dress, sewn by her aunt Mary before she left them for her new life in Florida.

I'm glad you're doing this, Adam, his sister had told him. *You need a woman in your home again—a wife of your own.*

Everyone had been of the same opinion, and watching Verna and Amanda Rebecca together, he knew they were right. The home needed this. His daughter needed a proper *mamm*. And he…well, he wasn't sure if he really deserved a wife, but here he was with a proper woman ready to put her touch on his home, and he was grateful.

Verna would fit in here…in time. It would take some adjustment, of course. But he could already see the happy influence she would be around here. And maybe he could find some of those old family connections from his grandfather's day in Redemption. They'd all settle in and find their place.

"Okay, the hot chocolate is done," Verna said. "Where are the mugs, Amanda Rebecca?"

"I'll get them!"

Adam hadn't seen a smile like that on his daughter's face in quite some time. She went to the counter and grabbed the mugs, bringing two of them to Verna at the stove.

"Do you have a ladle?" Verna asked.

His daughter hurried off again, hauling open a drawer and fishing around inside for a moment before she emerged with one. She slammed shut the drawer and came back to the stove.

"No slamming," Adam said.

"Sorry, Daet."

Verna dipped the ladle into the pot and filled the first mug.

"Take that to your *daet*," she said, casting a smile over her shoulder.

Amanda Rebecca carried the mug carefully to where Adam sat at the table. She set it down in front of him.

"It's hot chocolate," she announced with a beaming smile. "And I helped. Did you see, Daet? I helped."

"I did see," he replied.

"This is yours, Amanda," Verna called.

Amanda Rebecca. That was her name. He'd called her by her full name since she was born. He wouldn't correct Verna, though. He'd mention it later, perhaps. They both looked too happy for him to ruin it.

Amanda Rebecca collected her mug of hot chocolate and carried it carefully to the table, her gaze fixed on the cup with concentration. Then Verna filled her own mug with the last of the contents in the pot, and she joined them both at the table.

Adam took a sip. "Mmm."

"Do you like it, Daet?" his daughter asked, and she blew on the surface of the drink, then took a little sip, too. "Oh, it *is* good. This is even better than Aunt Mary's."

"I should be careful." Verna looked down

at the front of her dress and at her sleeves. "I should have changed out of my dress into something I wouldn't mind getting dirty."

Her dress was spotless. She wore a gray work apron over the top of it. That gray apron had been an absolute necessity, his mother had told him. So he'd hung it on a hook next to the counter.

"Will you wear your dress every church Sunday?" Amanda Rebecca asked.

"*Yah*. Every one. I have to take very good care of it."

Amish women wore their blue wedding dresses to service every other Sunday when the community worshipped together. Until the dress started to wear out, and then she'd put it neatly away in her hope chest.

He'd seen Verna's hope chest when her father and brother-in-law delivered it that morning. They'd carried it upstairs, and he'd pointed out her bedroom. There had been an awkward pause when they realized her room would not be his. He'd had to explain it was upon her request, but he knew that they were wondering already what kind of marriage this would be.

It would be a respectful one. And a kind one. And none of their business.

Still…he was looking forward to finding

out what little treasures she'd put away into her hope chest over the years for her married home. He hadn't lifted the lid. It was hers.

Verna settled into the chair opposite him, his daughter perched on the seat between them. Amanda Rebecca put her attention into blowing on her hot chocolate and sipping it slowly so that it left a little brown rim around her lips.

"Could I ask you a question?" Verna said.

"*Yah*. Of course."

"You mentioned before that your family came from Redemption, a long time ago," she said.

"*Yah*, they did. My great-great-grandfather settled a farm here. He cleared all the trees himself, picked all the rocks out of the soil... everything. That was a long time ago. His son inherited the land, and then my grandfather left for Oregon, and the rest is history."

"So the farm is still in your family?" she asked.

He shook his head. "No, I don't know the details, but it seems to have been sold to someone else. I actually found out by contacting one of the registry agents in Oregon. They were able to get the information from Pennsylvania for me. It's a little farm quite close to town. The old man who owns it just got married, I believe," he replied.

"Moe Stoltzfus?" Verna asked.

"*Yah*, that's the man."

"He just got married a couple of months ago to my good friend's grandmother," she said. "And it's his farm that your family owned all those years ago?"

"That's the one," Adam replied.

"He moved next door, to his wife's house. Her house was more suited to elderly people," she said.

"So he isn't living on that land?" he asked, an idea suddenly sparking.

"No, not right now. The house is empty."

"I had hoped to see the place, just for my own personal interest. My great-great-grandparents were buried on that land. My grandfather told me that much. I wanted to find their graves, if it was possible."

"I'm sure Moe would let you look around," she replied.

"I'm sure he would," Adam replied. "But honestly? If Moe isn't living on the land, do you think he might let me buy it? I mean, with my family's history there, we'd surely treasure it."

Verna nodded slowly. "Maybe he would. It's hard to tell."

"He must have children, though," Adam said. "Do they live around here? Someone who'd inherit the place?"

"He has one son in Ohio," Verna said. "And another two sons in Indiana."

"So no one...local." Adam couldn't help the hope rising inside of him.

"No, they all had to move. You know how hard it is to get Amish Pennsylvania farmland these days."

It was incredibly hard. His family had settled out in Oregon for a reason—the farmland was easier to come by, and family could settle near each other. "Verna, as you know, I was helping my brother run the farm in Oregon, and I'll inherit half of that land eventually."

"*Yah*, you told me," she said. "And you also promised that we would settle here in Redemption."

"Of course," he said quickly. "I'm not going back on my word."

She smiled faintly.

"The thing is, it isn't a large farm. After Rebecca died, I was able to work with my brother easily enough and eat at their table. But it might be nice to buy a farm of our own. Maybe even one where I have some family history. What would you think of that?"

"Are you asking me?" Verna asked.

"*Yah*. I am," he replied.

Verna straightened. "Our first serious financial discussion as a married couple."

"Also our first mug of hot chocolate as a married couple." He shot her a smile.

"All right, well…" Verna seemed to be rolling the proposal around in her mind. "I like the idea of having a farm of our own. But it might be hard to get the place from Moe. We could try, though."

Adam nodded. "You might help me."

"How?" she asked.

"You know people here. I don't."

"I know Moe quite well," she said. "And while it might make logical sense for him to sell it, old men can be attached to their land."

Adam sighed. It might very well be too much to hope that he could pass a legacy down to Amanda Rebecca, and to their children that would come later.

"Let's see what we can do," Adam said. "You never know what doors Gott will open."

"Very true." Verna smiled. "He opened this one for us to get married, didn't He?"

Amanda Rebecca drained her mug of hot chocolate, and Verna passed her a napkin.

"I'll get her ready for bed," Verna said.

"*Yah*, that would be a very nice start, don't you think, Amanda Rebecca?" he asked.

His daughter looked up at Verna uncertainly. "My *daet* helps me wash my face."

"What if I helped?" Verna asked. "I'll even tuck you in, and your *daet* can come give you a kiss—"

"That's not how it works," she said. "Daet tells me to sleep well and I go to bed."

"You don't get tucked in?"

The girl shook her head, and Adam suddenly felt a little rush of regret. He'd been trying to teach her how to be a big girl and to be strong. Had he been wrong there?

"Well, if you don't mind, I'd like to tuck you in," Verna said. "It's time to talk to each other and get an extra hug."

Amanda Rebecca's cheeks pinked, and she nodded.

Adam listened that evening as Verna tucked his daughter into bed. He heard the murmur of voices, and when he climbed the stairs, he saw the soft glow of kerosene light under the door. Then the door opened and she came in the hallway with the lamp in her hand.

"Good night. Dream sweet dreams," Verna said softly.

And Adam stood there, knowing in his heart that Verna had brought a very special kind of love into this home, but he didn't know how it might look between himself and Verna.

"Good night, Amanda Rebecca," he called.

"Night night, Daet!" came the little voice from her room.

He stood still for a moment, then cleared his throat. "*Danke* for being so kind to her."

"I will love her with all my heart." Verna's eyes misted. "I wanted *kinner* of my own for a very long time. And I truly believe that Amanda Rebecca is the start of Gott answering my prayer."

How blessed was he? Adam knew it.

"Well…" He swallowed. "Did you want to do anything this evening?"

"I'm actually a little tired," she said.

"*Yah*. I see. You would be." He nodded a couple of times.

"Aren't you tired?" she asked.

No, he wasn't at all. He was a little wired, actually. He'd just gotten married today, and his thoughts and feelings were twisted and jumbled inside of him.

"Uh… Not as tired as you," he said. "Feel free to go to bed, if you like. I won't stop you. In fact, I'll clean up the last few dishes in the kitchen."

"The dishes!" Verna's eyes widened. "I'll do it—"

"I won't hear of it," he replied. "I intend to be a considerate husband. You go rest. I'm happy to do it."

Verna moved toward her bedroom, and Adam stood there awkwardly. A woman in the house…a *wife* in the house… This was going to take some getting used to.

He went down the stairs slowly, and her bedroom door creaked and then shut with a click. He looked over his shoulder one more time as he descended the stairs.

Adam's first marriage hadn't been easy. They'd loved each other so dearly, and they both seemed to get their feelings hurt constantly. Especially Rebecca. And then he'd feel like a fool, and not even know exactly what he'd done wrong. But he'd let her down, somehow, and as a young husband that had been the biggest feeling of failure. It was worse when she went to her parents for help in sorting out their issues. And then the bishop had somehow gotten entangled… He didn't ever want to feel that way again. He'd be careful, polite, considerate. And he wouldn't allow his own emotions to get raw and affected.

Adam and Verna were starting their life in a more reasonable, measured way. He'd consult her on financial matters. He'd be flexible with her knitting classes, and he thought this more cautious course was wise.

But the memory of Marvin Kauffman's face when he found out about those separate bedrooms left a little nagging doubt in his heart.

It *was* wise…wasn't it?

Chapter Three

The next morning, Verna woke up to the sound of movement in the kitchen below. She picked up her watch in the dim morning light and saw that she'd overslept by half an hour. It was already five.

She got up, shivering in the chilly bedroom, and quickly got into her nearly new purple cape dress, thick black tights and a thick charcoal-gray cardigan she'd knitted herself. This was her first full day as a wife, and she had duties of her own. How had she slept so long? Maybe it was just the exhaustion of a wedding day catching up with her, but today was the first morning she'd woken up a married woman, and she would not be falling down on her duties now.

She went to the mirror, found her brush and brushed her long, brown hair, then twisted it up into a bun at the back of her head and pinned it in place. She paused to look at her face—not so young as she used to be. She'd never been considered a great beauty, not that the Amish put much stock in such things. In fact, she'd never put much stock in such things until now that she had a husband to please. She had noticed some lines starting around her eyes.

"That's vanity," she murmured to herself.

But Adam was no younger than she was. They'd just have to age together. That was what marriage was about, wasn't it?

Verna pulled on her white *kapp* that fit over her bun, the strings hanging down behind her back. Vanity needed to be set aside.

She brushed her teeth, washed her face and then headed down the stairs into the kitchen. *Her kitchen.* It still felt like a bit of a dream. This old kitchen would be hers to organize and run as she saw fit, and today she could start on that. She spotted the mugs and pot from last night's hot chocolate, washed and waiting in the dishrack to be put away.

Adam's back was to her, and he squatted in front of the woodstove, a small, orange flame already visible over his shoulder in the depths of the stove's belly.

"I'm sorry I slept in," she said.

Adam turned, shutting the stove door. "It's okay."

"I'm normally up promptly at four thirty," she said. "It won't happen again."

"I'm used to fixing my own breakfast and getting a lunch together," he said. "I used to leave before my sister woke up in the morning."

"Well, you won't be doing that anymore," Verna said. "A sister might not wake up that early for you, but your wife certainly will. That's for me to do."

"Danke." He smiled. "I do appreciate it. She's looking forward to meeting you, you know."

"I'm looking forward to meeting her, too." Verna went into the kitchen and pulled some bacon and sausage out of the ice box. "How do you like your eggs?"

He eyed her hesitantly. "I don't want to be a bother."

"Try me."

"Well... I like them fried on both sides, but just a little runny in the center. Not completely runny, but runny enough in the middle that when you cut them open, it drips onto the plate. It's okay. I know it's picky. I can make them myself."

"That's called over easy, and I'll just let

them cook a few seconds longer," she said. "It's no problem."

"No?"

"No." She went to the stove and added another two pieces of wood, then opened the burner cover with a hook. "How does Amanda like hers?"

"Amanda Rebecca," he said.

"Right." She smiled faintly. "It's just such a mouthful, Adam. Her friends will shorten it, you know."

"But I will not," Adam replied. "Her name is Amanda Rebecca."

So he wouldn't budge on that. Verna nodded.

"Okay, Adam."

She put a pat of butter onto the skillet, and it sizzled and slid from the center toward the side of the pan. Then she reached for the sausages. One word of wisdom her mother had given her before she left the bishop's house was that a man was much more willing to bend his views when his stomach was full. It looked like she'd need all the old wives' wisdom she could get, because she was now a new wife, and life was going to be interesting!

That evening, Verna had her knitting class. As he promised, Adam was home in plenty of time to eat the dinner she'd prepared so that she could clean up the dishes and then put on her coat, boots and gloves and head out into the cold, winter night as she'd done for the better part of the last year. She enjoyed teaching this class, and the young English-ers who attended had become an important part of her life.

There was comfort in sitting alone in the buggy, the reins in her hands. This was a different buggy than she'd driven at her parents' home. This was Adam's—he had two. There was the big covered buggy, and a small two-seater buggy that was open to the air. Considering the cold, they'd agreed she'd take this larger one. The familiarity of driving down country roads toward Redemption's community center brought a certain relief. As happy as she was to be officially married and have a little girl of her own to care for, she needed something familiar that was hers alone.

Is that selfish of me, Gott? she prayed.

Maybe it was. But she did need a little bit of space to be the same Verna she'd always been.

The community center was located on the east side of the town, beyond the touristy center of Amish shops. It was tucked between the local high school and junior high school, just beyond some streets of squat little houses with cars and pickup trucks parked on the street outside of them.

Everything looked prettier with a fresh mantle of snow on top of it, and as Verna pulled into the buggy parking at the far end of the lot, she couldn't help but smile at the twinkling little lights the management had strung up above the hitching post.

She gathered her cloth bag of knitting supplies, put a blanket over the horse's back to keep her warm and then paused to pet her nose.

"You and I will be good friends before long," she assured the big mare.

Then she headed over to the sidewalk that had been neatly shoveled and walked briskly toward the cheery lights of the little building. She pulled open the main door, and the murmuring voices of the AA group that met there at the same time came from a door that was propped open.

"Hi, my name is Tom, and I'm an alcoholic…"

"Hi, Tom…"

Verna had been raised with a distrust for Englisher ways. In fact, she'd had a few biases before this job blew them apart. She had to admire the Englisher determination to face their problems and recover. Like the teens she taught at her knitting class. She didn't think any at-risk Englisher youth would care a fig about knitting. In fact, most hadn't cared at all when they started, but her beginner knitting class was part of their court-ordered payment for some misdemeanor crime. Shoplifting, damage to public property, that sort of thing. And the judge had mandated that they learn to knit. Of all things!

But that was the point of these classes—to introduce some work ethic and general moral uprightness to these young people who might never have seen it before. Plus, Verna was paid for her time.

Verna opened the door to her little classroom at the end of the hall. She left it open and put her bag down on a chair. Then she began moving the chairs into a circle, as she always did when she first arrived. The circle was important.

They knitted together. They talked. They were equals here. She wasn't above them, and they weren't above her. Like a crafting circle of Amish women, except her students weren't all girls, and none were Amish.

"Hi, Miss Verna."

Verna looked up to see her first student come into the room. Her legal name was Cherie, but she didn't answer to anything but Blade.

Like a blade of grass? Verna had asked hopefully.

Sure... And that had made Blade smile. It was the start of a unique friendship.

"Hi, Blade," Verna said, casting her a smile. "How was your week?"

"Not bad," the girl replied. She dropped a backpack beside a chair. The bag was always stuffed full—and it didn't look like school books. She wore black jeans and a black leather jacket that didn't seem half warm enough for the weather. "How was yours?"

"Good." She couldn't help the grin that suddenly came to her face.

"Oh, that good, huh?" Blade gave her a curious look. "What happened?"

"Well..." This was the first time Verna was going to tell someone who didn't already know. "I got married yesterday."

"Wait...yesterday? Like twenty-four hours ago?"

"Yah."

"Congrats." Blade shook her head. "I didn't even know you had a boyfriend. Talk about keeping secrets."

"I didn't have a boyfriend," Verna replied. "I wasn't holding out on you."

That was one thing she'd discovered with this group. They might have problems keeping the law, but they took honesty between friends seriously, and "holding out" with important information was seen as a betrayal.

"Then how did you get married?" Blade asked.

"We have a matchmaker in our community," Verna said. "She found a man who she thought would be a good match for me, and she was right. We got married yesterday."

"A good match, how?" Blade demanded.

"His name is Adam Lantz, and he needed a wife. He has a little girl who's four years old and needs a mother to take care of her," Verna said. "And with me being just about thirty… Well…"

"So ancient." Blade rolled her eyes.

"Well, I wanted to be married, and this was my chance," Verna said, feeling a little defensive. The thing was, this was a fast marriage in Amish eyes, too. Everyone blinked a couple of times when they found out how quickly they'd moved.

"Sorry. I'm not trying to be a pain. It's just…wow."

"Yah," Verna chuckled. "For me, too."

"Are you quitting, then?" Blade eyed her warily.

"This class?" Verna asked, placing the last chair where it belonged. "Of course, not! I

might bring my stepdaughter with me sometimes, though."

"Oh... Okay, good." Blade slouched into
a chair, opened her bag and pulled out her
knitting needles.

The rest of the class started to arrive then,
one at a time. Jolene, Tia, Abigail and finally
Harry. Harry was the one boy who came—
he'd told her it was better than time in juve-
nile hall. He was thin, with constant rings
under his eyes, and he always inspired the
desire inside of Verna to feed him. It was because of Harry and that hungry look about
him that she'd begun bringing snacks with
her to feed these *kinner*.

"Verna got married yesterday," Blade announced.

"What?" Tia whirled around. She was a
petite girl with hair growing out a bleached
blonde dye job—roots dark brown. "Miss
Verna, you got married?"

"I did," she said.

"To who?" Harry demanded.

She told them the same thing she'd told
Blade.

"Just like that?" Tia said. "What if you
don't like him?"

"But I do like him," Verna replied.

"What if he ends up being mean, or something?" Abigail asked. "My mom has come across plenty of losers. Trust me on that."

"We have a matchmaker who looks into his character before anyone even suggests a meeting," Verna said. "My new husband came highly recommended by his own community in Oregon. And I liked him very much when I met him. And he…well, he liked me."

"That's not enough," Tia said bluntly. "He *liked* you? He'd better downright worship you."

"It'll have to be enough," Verna said, starting to feel irritated. "Because we are married now. And we only worship Gott. So I don't expect that from him. But I do expect kindness, and honesty, and some gentleness."

"And you're…happy?" That was from Abigail, and she sat down in her chair, eyeing Verna suspiciously.

"*Yah.* Of course."

"Then what are you doing here?" Blade asked.

The room fell silent, and Verna swallowed hard. She could tell them something that sounded upright and holy, but this particular group wouldn't buy it. They always said they could smell horse poop a mile away—their words, not hers—and she had learned to believe them. They didn't accept half-truths—not in the knitting circle.

"I'm… I'm here because I like this class. Okay?" Verna felt a lump rise in her throat. "I like all of you. I enjoy knitting together and talking, and if I didn't come today, then the chances of everything changing and me never being able to come again was far too high. All right? That's why!"

Verna's hands trembled, and she pressed her palms against her abdomen. That was more honest than she'd been with anyone in the last two weeks. Because they were right— this marriage had been quick, and if Verna hadn't just jumped into it like this, she might have talked herself out of it.

"Fair enough," Harry said, sliding into his seat. "Let us know if he gets out of line. We'll sort him out for you."

"I don't need that," Verna said, and she smiled shakily.

"Don't change for him, okay?" Abigail said. "My mom turns into a different person for every guy she's with. I hate it. And I like you the way you are. So don't go and change on us."

"I will do my best not to," Verna said, then she pulled her own knitting from her bag.

"Congratulations on your wedding," Harry said.

The others murmured their own polite

words, and Verna sank into her seat. Who would have thought that telling this group about her marriage would be the toughest? Maybe she should have guessed.

"How far did you all get on your scarves this week?" Verna asked. This was a knitting class, after all.

Then her little class of at-risk teens pulled out their handiwork. None were very good at this. Their scarves were of varying lengths. Jolene's scarf was turning out rather well. Tia's had odd little holes all over it where she'd dropped stitches and picked up new ones. Abigail's scarf had started out quite narrow and just kept getting wider and wider as she picked up new stitches and didn't seem to know how. Harry's scarf moved along at a snail's pace, only six inches long after he'd been working on it for a month already. And Blade's scarf was knitted so tightly that it could hardly even be called a piece of knitting at all. It was so tight that every single class without exception, Blade snapped the yarn and had to tie it together again. But she kept going, jamming her needle under the thread, with a squeak.

"You're doing so well!" Verna said, smiling at them. "I'm so glad you keep coming."

"It's either this or juvie," Harry muttered.

"Well, I have a choice, and I choose all of you," Verna replied.

They talked as they worked, and Verna went around the room and give them tips and hints about how to make the knitting easier. But she never, ever criticized the knitting they had done already. Because it was precious— the earnest, early attempts of young people who were learning to apply themselves to a difficult task. Those tight, awkward stitches were a thing of absolute beauty.

And she had to wonder… Would Adam understand?

Adam stood in Amanda Rebecca's doorway, hesitating. His daughter crawled into her bed and pulled her blankets up over her shoulders. She gave a little shiver and rolled over onto her side.

"Daet?"

"*Yah*, Amanda Rebecca?"

"Is it only a *mamm* or an *aent* who tucks *kinner* into bed?"

His sister had taken over the motherly role with his daughter, and he hadn't thought about being the one to do it. It seemed too gentle, somehow.

"Oh…well…." He wasn't sure what to say. "Should I tuck you in?"

"Yah."

He went into the room and stood next to her bed. He bent down a little awkwardly and adjusted the blankets. Did that count as tucking? He wasn't even sure.

"Say your prayer," he said.

"Dear Gott, take care of me as I sleep tonight, and give me good dreams," she said.

"Amen." Adam paused. "Why good dreams?"

"I had a scary dream last night," she said.

"What did you dream?"

"That you went away, and I was all by myself," she said.

If only she could understand how impossible that was. He'd gotten married for his daughter's future. He'd turned his entire life upside down so that she'd have a mother to take care of her.

"I won't ever go away," he said.

"Really?"

"Really."

"You won't leave me with Verna and go do big grown-up man things?" she asked.

"I'll go to work, but I'll always come home to you, Amanda Rebecca. I didn't marry Verna so that I could leave you with her. I'll never do that."

"Do you promise?"

"Yah. I promise."

"Okay, then."

Outside the window, he heard the clop of hooves. Would that be Verna returning from her knitting class? He headed over to the window and looked out. *Yah*, that was his buggy and horse. He'd expressed some worry about her traveling alone at night, and she'd told him that she'd done it on her own all this time, and that she'd be fine. All the same, it was a relief to know she'd returned safely.

Adam went back to his daughter's bed, smoothed a hand over her glossy, blond hair and then planted a kiss on the top of her head.

"Good night," he said.

"Is that Verna come home?" she asked.

"*Yah*, it is. And you must call her Mamm."

"Can... Mamm...come tuck me in, too?"

He felt a little pang in his heart. She was accepting Verna—that was a good thing. But he'd no longer be his daughter's sun and moon, would he? If all went well, Verna would step into a mother's role, and he'd... step back.

"Of course," he said. "Now, I have to go help her unhitch."

That was a husband's duty, to help his wife unhitch and take care of the men's work around a place. He jogged down the stairs, grabbed his coat and plunged his feet into his boots. He headed outside and got to the buggy just as Verna had gotten down.

"How was your class?" Adam asked.

"Good. Very good." She smiled.

"What do you do with them?" he asked. "Just knit?"

"It's more than knitting. We talk, too. I just told them I got married. They were deeply offended they didn't know about it earlier, and when I explained how we...well, how our arrangement came to be, I don't think they understood."

She was talking about their personal business with a group of Englisher teens?

"Why should you explain anything?" he asked with a frown. "It isn't exactly their business."

And he and Verna were well and truly married. If a group of Englisher teens didn't like it, it shouldn't matter. But he cared how it made Verna feel.

"Would you rather I not tell them I got married?" Her eyebrows rose. She certainly had no shyness about confronting him, did she?

"No," he admitted. "I just don't like being judged by a group of Englishers, I suppose."

"We should probably get used to that." She smiled faintly. "It was good practice anyway.

We'll have to tell a lot of people about our wedding."

But the Amish wouldn't judge them. They'd see the practicality of the union and wish them well. Adam went over to the horse and started to undo buckles.

"They're a good group of *kinner*," Verna said. "They're protective of me. They care."

"I care, too," he said. "I don't like my wife risking her safety at night on these roads."

"Oh, Adam," she said with a smile. "That's sweet, but I'm thirty, and I've fended for myself all this time. I'm fine. I can drive that buggy as well as anyone."

But he'd learned firsthand that women were more fragile than he'd ever guessed when he lost his first wife. She'd died from complications of a bad flu—something he'd never expected to be a danger. And add to that, they had a little girl in their own home who needed Verna, too, and he wished that Verna would see that she belonged there, with them, not out teaching a bunch of Englisher young people how to use knitting needles. Still, Adam had agreed to this, and even if he wanted to protect her in the only ways he knew how, he wouldn't go back on his word.

"I'll take care of the horse," Adam said. "You can go on inside where it's warm. I just put Amanda Rebecca to bed. She asked if you'd tuck her in, too."

"Really?" Verna's voice softened. "She asked for me?"

"She did."

"That's encouraging." Verna nodded quickly. "*Danke*, Adam. I'll go and see her, then."

Verna paused at his side, and he looked down at her. His wife. He wanted to reach out and touch her cheek…or take her hand… but as soon as he'd thought of it, she'd turned away again and started off across the snow toward the house.

He worked quickly to unhitch the horse and then led her into the stable. He brushed her down, gave her some oats and then touched her soft muzzle.

"Things will certainly be different," he told the horse. "And in all the best ways."

He pulled the stable door shut behind him and headed back toward the house. When he got inside, he hung up his coat next to Verna's and took off his boots. He could hear soft voices coming from Amanda Rebecca's bedroom, and he went up the staircase toward them.

He didn't mean to listen in, exactly, but he had been curious about how Verna was bonding with his little girl. It was only right and responsible for him to make sure it was going well between them.

He paused on the landing. There was a kerosene light on in his daughter's room, and the door stood ajar.

"Did you have fun tonight?" Amanda Rebecca's voice sounded a little tired.

"I did," Verna said. "I enjoy knitting. I'm going to knit you a little sweater. Maybe a nice black one you can wear to Service Sunday to keep you warm."

"And maybe a pink one, to match my dress?"

"*Yah.* I could do that, too."

"Is it hard to knit?"

"Not especially, once you learn how it works. Would you like to learn?" Silence, but there must have been a nod because Verna said, "Okay. I'll start teaching you. That would be fun for me, too."

"What do they call you in your knitting class?" Amanda Rebecca asked. "Do they call you Teacher?"

"They call me Miss Verna. It's the way Englishers show respect."

"They should call you Teacher."

"Maybe." A soft laugh.

"Can I tell you a secret?" Amanda Rebecca asked. "The girls at Service Sunday don't call me Amanda Rebecca."

Adam's heart skipped a beat.

"What do they call you?" Verna asked.

"Mandy." The word was so soft that Adam almost didn't make it out.

"Oh…that's cute, isn't it?"

"I like it," Amanda Rebecca said. "Can you call me Mandy, too?"

"I—" Silence again. "I don't think your *daet* likes that."

"Oh…"

"I'm sorry, little one."

They were bonding, all right. They were doing just fine, and he was already disappointing the both of them. Adam turned and headed quietly down the stairs.

He stood at the bottom and felt a wave of frustration. He wasn't a cruel man. He had reasons for all of his requests—good reasons.

But he'd wanted a *mamm* for his daughter, and now he had one. How much was going to change around here? Maybe he should be grateful, but deep down he felt a well of rising loneliness. His little girl wasn't going to need him in the same way anymore, was she?

She had a *mamm* now.

Chapter Four

Verna ran a hand over Amanda Rebecca's hair and smiled at her. The girl's lids were heavy and she snuggled down into a fluffy pillow. The curtains were closed and the kerosene lamp burned softly from the top of the dresser. Amanda's Noah's Ark toy lay on the bed next to her, and she held a crocheted camel in one hand, stroking it with her thumb as if for comfort.

"Could you ask Daet if maybe, just maybe, I can be Mandy?" she asked. "Please?"

"I can ask, but he was very clear about that," Verna replied.

"Oh…"

"But maybe I could call you something else, just between the two of us," Verna suggested.

"You could call me Mandy?" She wasn't going to let go of this easily.

"No, but maybe I could call you honey."

"Okay." Amanda Rebecca's forehead wrinkled. "I think I like that. Can you still ask him about Mandy?"

"Yes, honey, I'll still ask him."

Amanda Rebecca smiled up at her. "I think I like that one. Should I call you honey, too?"

"No," Verna chuckled. "You can call me Mamm."

"Okay."

"Okay." Verna stroked her head once more, tempted to bend down and kiss her cheek, but somehow she didn't dare. Not quite yet. Things had gone so well that she was afraid of ruining them by rushing too fast.

"Night night."

Verna's heart gave a little squeeze as she looked down at the small girl. She made just a little lump under the quilt, and her pale hair spread over the pillow. So small, and so sweet.

"Night night," Verna said softly, and she dialed the wick of the kerosene lamp down until the light went out, then tiptoed out the door, shutting it softly behind her.

She and Amanda Rebecca would have a special relationship—she could feel it. Maybe it made a difference when a stepmother had saved up as much love inside of her as Verna had all those years of waiting. She'd tucked all her love away, waiting for a child of her own to spend it on. And now she had Amanda Rebecca... Verna sent up a silent prayer of thanks for this little stepdaughter. No, her *daughter*. She'd never refer to her as anything different. She was well and truly married now, and that made Amanda Rebecca her daughter.

Verna headed down the staircase and found her husband in the kitchen. He was leaning against the counter, a glass of water in front of him. His red-gold beard shone in the kerosene light of the lamp that hung overhead—but she could see the tension in his stiff shoulders.

"Thank you for taking care of the horse for me," Verna said. "I'm used to doing that myself."

"You have a husband now," Adam said, and he pressed his lips together. He turned away from her and pulled a bakery pack of muffins out of a cupboard. He held it out to her, and she accepted a blueberry muffin and peeled back the paper.

He did the same and left the package on the counter.

"How is Amanda Rebecca?" he asked.

"She's fine." She smiled. "It was nice that she wanted me to tuck her in. I think she and I will get along well."

"It looks that way," he said. "She seems to be warming to you."

"And I'm so happy about that," she replied. "Everyone hears about stepchildren who aren't so happy to have a new *mamm* in their home, and I was prepared to have to work a little harder for some acceptance from her."

"She's a good girl."

Verna nodded. "*Yah*. You've raised her very well, Adam. She's really quite wonderful."

And she meant it. Adam was quite stern and rigid, but his daughter was a wonderful child. Verna took a bite of the muffin. It was tasty, and she recognized the packaging from a local Amish bakery.

"I know I seem overly strict," Adam said, as if reading her mind.

"I didn't say—"

"I know. But I'm not. I have good reason for the things I require with my daughter."

She wished he'd said "our daughter," but he hadn't. He didn't think he was strict, but there was a little girl upstairs begging to be called a shortened version of her name, and he wouldn't allow it. Verna shifted her weight to her other foot and tried to paste on an accepting expression, although she wasn't sure she managed it because Adam's chewing slowed and he fixed her with a quizzical look.

"You disagree," he said, swallowing.

"Adam, I don't want to disrespect your late wife. I know you want to have her remembered through Amanda Rebecca, but sometimes children like having their names shortened," she said. "In fact, Amanda Rebecca said that the girls at Service Sunday call her Mandy for short, and she was hoping I could, too."

He didn't answer for a moment, and he put his unfinished muffin down on the counter. "I'm glad you told me that. I wasn't sure you would."

"You overheard?" She didn't exactly deserve privacy with his daughter, but she couldn't help but feel a little spied upon.

"I had just wanted to check that you were getting along." His cheeks colored a little bit. "If she was being rude to you or anything, I would have spoken to her about it."

"She isn't rude at all. She's very sweet," Verna countered.

"*Yah*, I heard." He nodded a couple of times.

"The thing is," Verna went on, "*kinner* will find nicknames for each other. It's part of building friendships."

When she was little, her father had called her Tadpole. And when she got older, the other girls had called her Vy. It was a shortened form of her own name. It had made her feel special, so she understood.

"It's also part of bullying," he countered.

She blinked up at him. "What?"

"I would know." Adam ran a hand over his beard, and his gaze flickered upward toward his daughter's bedroom, then back to Verna. "*Kinner* can be incredibly cruel with names—rhyming all sorts of insults together with a name. I don't want that to happen to Amanda Rebecca."

Verna's stomach dropped. "Have there been children who've bullied her?"

"Not her. But I've seen it happen." He straightened.

So there hadn't been any bullying toward her. Verna understood a father wanting to protect his little girl, but it seemed to her that Adam was taking this a little too far.

"But she *wants* to be called Mandy," she interjected.

"And I've said no." His tone firmed, and butterflies unsettled her stomach. Was this an argument? Amanda Rebecca was his daughter, and she knew that she was new here, but she also believed that Adam was wrong.

"Isn't it better to be vigilant and watch that no one is being mean?" she asked. "I understand that being difficult to do when you were raising her alone, but you have me now. I can keep an eye out and watch how the *kinner* play, how they talk to each other... I could talk to Amanda Rebecca about it, too—"

"Adults don't see it," he said tersely. "They can be very well-meaning. They can ask *kinner* about it and do their best to watch for it, but they don't see what's really happening between the *kinner.*"

But there was something in his voice that suggested he wasn't judging her abilities to supervise children. He dropped his gaze and crossed his arms over his chest. This went deeper.

"Was it you who was bullied?" she asked, lowering her voice.

"No, it was my younger brother Jonah," he said.

"What happened?"

"Some Englisher boys started rhyming his name with some crude things, and they wouldn't stop. They kept pestering him," he replied. "It was awful for him—worse than anyone realized. I knew what was happening, but my parents didn't. I told Jonah to just ignore them. And he tried, but it's much harder for *kinner.* I thought ignoring them was easy. It wasn't for him."

"I'm sorry," she said. "That's awful for a little boy to go through. What made them stop?"

"He died."

Verna's heart hammered to a stop in her chest, and she stared at him. "Your brother died?"

"*Yah*. It was the middle of winter. He was running away from them, and he went out onto a frozen pond. It was a man-made pond, the kind that is used for runoff water. There was a pocket of air between the ice and the water, and he went through it. We couldn't get him back out again in time."

"Adam…" she breathed.

"So… I know what I'm talking about. Teasing and bullying can go too far. It doesn't matter that the boys felt terrible. Their parents came to our farm and offered their sincere apologies. They assured us that their sons had learned their lesson. The boys were in tears, and they held a memorial service in town since we didn't invite them to the Amish funeral. As adults, one of the boys—now a man—sought me out and told me again how terrible he felt about that accident. But none of that could bring Jonah back."

Verna had nothing to say. She just looked at him, her breath bated.

"When Amanda Rebecca was born, I promised myself that she'd have a name that rhymed with absolutely nothing," he said fiercely. "And nothing does rhyme with Amanda Rebecca, does it?"

A shuffle on the stairs drew Verna's gaze, and she spotted Amanda Rebecca standing there in her little white nightgown that was a little too short on her legs and arms.

"What's going on?" the girl asked, her eyes wide.

"Nothing, honey," Verna said. "Your *daet* was just telling me a story."

"About me?" Her voice quavered. She must have heard her name.

"No, honey," Verna said. "Come, I'll put you back to bed."

"Everything is fine, Amanda Rebecca," Adam said. "Go to bed. Morning comes soon enough."

"Are you allowed to call me honey?" the girl asked gravely, her gaze moving over toward her father for permission.

"Of course, I am," Verna said with some forced brightness, loud enough for Adam to hear her clearly. "You are like a little golden drop of honey. You make everything sweeter."

But she looked over at Adam, too, hoping he wouldn't contradict her. He didn't. Instead he headed over to the coats, put his on and pushed his feet into his boots. As Verna led Amanda Rebecca back up the stairs, the door opened, a whoosh of cold air whisked inside and then it shut again solidly.

"Is Daet mad at me?" Amanda Rebecca whispered.

"No, honey, he isn't. He's just—" But what was Adam feeling? Was he upset about his little brother? Was he upset with Verna? And just walking out like that had left her heart hovering in her middle, too.

"He's what?" Amanda Rebecca asked.

"You know what?" Verna said. "I honestly don't know what he's feeling. But I'm going to ask him. I'm going to find out. Okay?"

"You can do that?" the girl whispered.

"Of course, I can," she said brightly. "That is what *mamms* are for."

Although that came out of her mouth before she'd even thought it through. *Mamms* were not for contradicting the *daets*. They were supposed to be the constant, loving support in the home. They were supposed to be silently and stalwartly aligned with their husbands, backing them up and creating a united front for the children.

And yet, this little girl needed someone to tell her that everything would be okay, and then make sure that it would be. The complication in this marriage was not her step-daughter, it was her new husband.

How on earth was she supposed to connect with him?

Adam marched out into the snow, his heart hammering in his chest. He hadn't meant to bring up Jonah, and for some reason that memory of his brother disappearing under the ice had come back with the strength of a thunderclap. He shivered, and it had nothing to do with the cold outside, either. His chest felt tight, and his breath came shallow. He had to stand for a couple of minutes, sucking cold air into his lungs until he felt that helpless, spinning sensation ebbing away.

He held his lantern up, the soft, golden light spreading ahead of him. The frigid air was bracing, and his heartbeat started to slow. It had been a long time ago, and he hadn't had an episode like this in years. Why now?

The memory of that broken ice returned again, and he pushed it back as forcefully as he could. Remembering it didn't change anything. But he'd had to explain himself to Verna, because otherwise he looked like an inflexible tyrant, which he wasn't.

Adam looked back toward the house. The light from the kitchen shone comfortingly, and up in Amanda Rebecca's bedroom another light bobbed around, then went out. She'd be back in bed now.

He angled his steps toward the stable. There was always some bit of work that needed doing in there—a horse that could be brushed, tools to be organized, hay troughs to be refilled. Although when he opened the door and stepped inside, he just stood there.

He'd messed that up. He could feel it. Amanda Rebecca had been unsettled, and while Verna seemed to handle it just fine, he felt like the outsider, which was a strange feeling with his own daughter.

He walked down the stable aisle to where his horse stood, blinking sleepily at him. He pet the animal's muzzle and felt his own tension release. Footsteps crunched in the snow outside the door, and then it opened and he turned to see Verna step inside, the door bouncing shut after her.

For a moment she just looked at him, her mouth open and her eyes glistening with repressed emotion. Then she said, "Can I say something?"

"Yah." He stepped away from the horse and eyed her warily. He'd been married before, and he knew what an angry woman looked like, except his first wife used to keep

to the kitchen when she was mad. And she'd refuse to talk to him.

"You can't do that." Her voice shook, and she gulped in a breath.

"What, exactly?" he asked. He wasn't trying to be smart with her—he needed to know.

"You got upset, and then you stomped out," she said.

It wasn't exactly what had happened. It wasn't anger that had driven him from the house, but a suffocating squeezing in his chest.

"I'm not upset," he said, calming his voice.

"And don't do that, either," she said. "Don't say you aren't upset when you obviously are. We're very newly married, Adam, and I want to be a good wife to you, but you don't know what that just did to me and Amanda Rebecca."

"She's in bed, isn't she?"

"*Yah,* she's back in bed, but she's afraid that you're mad at her."

His heart sank. "I'm not mad at her…"

"But you *acted* mad at her."

Adam closed the distance between them and stopped a couple of feet away from her. He wished he could hug her, but since he'd not hugged her yet, starting now seemed wrong.

So instead, he just stood there, looking at her red, cold hands.

"I realize you are probably mad at *me*," she added, her voice low. "And I apologize for upsetting you."

"I'm not mad at you, either," he said, and her gaze flickered up toward him uncertainly.

"No?"

"No, I—" He sucked in a breath. "It hasn't happened in a long time, but sometimes when I remember my brother's death, I... I feel like I'm drowning. I don't know how else to explain it. I feel...panicked."

"Oh." Her gaze was fixed on his face now, and her brow was furrowed. "I'm sorry."

"It's not your fault. I had to explain about what happened to him, and..." He sighed. "I needed air. It wasn't anger." But that wasn't entirely true. "I was a little angry, but—"

She didn't answer him, and Adam let the words hang in the air. There was more than panic and anger drifting away. There was another feeling deep inside that he couldn't quite identify, but that he wanted to flush out as quickly as possible, too.

"—that doesn't happen often," he added.

"Okay." She nodded, but she still looked hesitant.

"You should just say it—whatever it is that you're holding back," he said.

It would be easier that way, instead of him trying to guess at what she was thinking. And he didn't think he could handle that look on her face every time she glanced his way.

"I was advised to keep my feelings to myself in the first few months of marriage," she said.

Ah. The advice given to young wives…and perhaps to wives married to men they hardly knew. He understood the reason behind it, but it wasn't what he wanted.

"I want to tell you something, but I want it to stay private between us," Adam said. "Can I trust you to keep this confidence?"

"*Yah*, Adam. Of course."

Since he was explaining himself today, he might as well get it over with.

"When I got married to Rebecca, she wasn't happy," he said. "I tried to do everything I could to please her, but it wasn't enough. We hurt each other's feelings a lot. We didn't mean to, but we did."

"How long did you court?" she whispered.

"Two years. So it wasn't like…us." He saw the faint wince as he said the words. "Anyway, the point is, when she got upset with me, she would go to her parents and she'd tell them what I'd done. And they'd help her to feel better and give her advice."

Verna nodded. She didn't see the problem, he realized—most women wouldn't.

"I should point out that she went to them with her hurt feelings instead of telling me," he amended.

"Oh!" Verna's expression sobered.

"*Yah*. It got to the point that there were too many people in our marriage. Her mother thought I should do things one way, and her father just thought I was letting them all down. I might have been able to sort that out over time, but then my wife went to the bishop."

"What had you done?" Verna breathed.

"Nothing awful," he said softly. "I...didn't meet her expectations, I suppose. But I've learned from that. And I won't make the same mistakes again."

And there had been plenty of mistakes. Things he said. Things he didn't say. Messes he'd left... But the biggest mistake was that he'd laid his heart out in front of Rebecca and then gotten hurt again and again. And he'd reacted in pain. Then she'd reacted, too. She'd loved him just as much as he'd loved her, and it didn't seem to help matters. In fact, it only made each of them more sensitive. That was a big reason why he'd preferred an arranged marriage. It would be more logical, less passionate. He'd be better this way, he was sure.

"The point is," he concluded, "if you are upset, I want you to tell me. Not your parents. Not the bishop. Me."

Verna nodded slowly.

"And maybe the advice to not share that with me was…well-meant, but misguided."

Verna licked her lips. "I can see that. All right. Then I will say it. When you marched out of the house, I felt terrible. It made the whole house cold. I didn't like that feeling of you just turning your back."

He'd made her feel that way by simply going outside? Women were complex creatures, weren't they? Had she preferred him to stand inside and struggle to breathe?

"Okay," Adam said carefully. "I can see that. I had thought our conversation was over."

She'd been heading upstairs to put Amanda Rebecca back to bed. Had she wanted him to wait for her to come back down?

"I would say our conversation isn't over until we feel better," she said.

That might make for some long conversations. He pulled off his hat and ran a hand through his hair.

"Okay," he said, and he had a sinking feeling that this marriage wasn't going to be so easy to navigate, either. "I'm sorry that I upset you, too."

A smile touched the corners of her lips. "*Danke*, Adam. I want us to be happy."

"Me, too." Desperately. Deeply. He longed for it, but he was starting to worry it wouldn't be so easy.

Those heavy emotions had lifted and drifted away, all but that last remaining feeling deep inside of him that left him so uneasy. It was a similar feeling to all those years ago when he'd lain on his belly on the ice, reaching into the numbing water, fumbling to grab on to something…anything.

Helpless.

That's what this feeling was. He felt helpless.

"I'm glad you want me to tell you things," she added. "It is reassuring."

"*Yah*, well… I'd rather you tell me," he said, suddenly feeling awkward.

"And I will promise you not to tell my parents or the bishop or anyone if I'm angry with you," she added. "I will tell you."

"*Danke*." That was a relief. At least he'd have a fighting chance of fixing it that way. Her forthrightness might be intimidating, but it was also a blessing. If a woman was too patient, her patience might run out at the worst time possible—with her friends, or with her family.

"Maybe I could make you a fried egg—just a little runny the way you like it—or a sandwich?" she asked hesitantly.

That was an olive branch. She wanted to make peace, and he nodded with a smile.

"That sounds very *gut*. I would like that."

What was it about a wife that made him feel so rampantly out of control? Because one smile like that one made him want to trail along after her back to the house. And he still didn't feel entirely confident in his abilities to keep her smiling.

Gott, guide me.

A good marriage was a comfort, they'd told him. He should try again. But a marriage to a good woman like Verna was also absolutely terrifying.

Chapter Five

Saturday morning, Verna, Amanda Rebecca and Adam made their way in their buggy toward the Stoltzfus home. Moe and Ellen had married late in life—both having lost their spouses—and they now lived in a house next door to Moe's farm.

Verna's friend Sarai had married Moe's grandson Arden, and they had moved to a fledgling Amish community in Ohio. Verna and Sarai wrote letters back and forth, sharing the local news with each other.

"Ellen Stoltzfus's granddaughter Sarai will be happy to know we visited them," Verna said. "In the same letter, I'll tell her that I got married, but honestly, I think Ellen will have already filled her in on that."

Adam smiled. "News travels fast."

"It does. But she'll want to hear about the wedding from me, of course."

Adam didn't answer. He rubbed the back of his neck, and when he dropped his hand again, he tapped a nervous rhythm on his knee.

"Are you all right?" she asked.

"*Yah.*"

"You seem…anxious."

He glanced over at her again. "I lost track of any family out here. My grandfather wasn't a very talkative man. He didn't say much about his life in Pennsylvania. And we certainly had no contact with any extended family out here. So…this is my first contact with anything connected to them."

"Why didn't he talk about his family?" she asked. "They didn't visit ever? He didn't write letters?"

"If he did, we didn't know it," Adam replied. "The only information I had was that he grew up on a farm outside of Redemption. That's it. And I got that from my father, not from my grandfather."

She looked out at the passing wintry fields. "I wonder what happened…"

"Me, too," he replied. "But this is a start."

She knew his *mamm* was an Englisher convert to the Amish faith, and she wondered if that had been difficult for him. Was it part of him not knowing as much as he should have about his Amish side of the family? Or was she being biased against Englishers again by even considering that? She felt her cheeks heat. She was a work in progress.

And who knew? Maybe Moe and Ellen would be happy to sell the farm. Maybe Moe's sons wouldn't want to come work it, and they'd be happier to have money to put into their own businesses elsewhere, and Adam would get that solid connection to his father's side of the family again. She sensed that he needed it, and on a bright, sunshiny winter morning almost anything seemed possible.

The Stoltzfus home was a cute little white house on a small acreage next to the Stoltzfus farm. And when they pulled in, Verna could see the rather lavish chicken coop visible in the back, and a few chickens were in the pen, pecking at the snowy ground in the brilliant sunlight. That large, new coop was from Sarai, who raised a flock of specialty hens. She'd moved most of the birds to Ohio where she was building up a new egg business, but there were a few quality layers left for her grandmother to care for, and which were now living in relative luxury.

"Amanda Rebecca, do you see that farm over there?" Adam said over his shoulder.

Amanda Rebecca popped up behind them and leaned forward for a better look. *"Yah?"*

"That used to belong to our family a long time ago. My great-grandfather—your great-*great*-grandfather—owned that farm."

"Oh…"

"Yah…" Adam leaned forward, his gaze moving over the land slowly. Verna could see the wistfulness in his eyes. That land spoke to him. He glanced at Verna. "Let's see how things stand."

Yes, they would see.

The side door opened and Moe came ambling outside, pulling on his coat. He was a slim, old man with a kindly smile and a black felt hat sitting straight across his forehead. He came carefully down the steps and waved.

"Good morning!" Moe called. "Beautiful day, isn't it?"

"Yah, very nice, very nice," Adam replied. "I wanted to come by and introduce myself. I'm Adam Lantz. Verna and I were recently married—"

"Of course," Moe said, coming up, and he cast a smile Verna's way. "Verna, dear girl, why don't you and the little one go on inside to see Ellen. She's been baking, and I know she'd love to serve you up some fresh apple cobbler.

Your husband and I will get the horses under the shelter with fresh hay."

Verna opened the buggy door and hopped down. She reached up for Amanda Rebecca and lowered her to the ground. She was as light as a barn cat. Adam hopped down, too, and he and Moe shook hands.

"So, you're from Oregon, are you?" Moe was saying as Verna and Amanda Rebecca headed past toward the side door. It opened with a flourish, and Ellen beamed at them. She was dressed in a gray cape dress with a crisp, white apron on top. She beckoned them to hurry and then slammed the door shut after them as they came into the mudroom.

"Come in, come in," Ellen said. "The stove is nice and warm. And what is your name?"

Amanda Rebecca cast Verna a sly little look. "Mandy."

"Mandy. What a sweet name. I have a sister named Amanda, and we called her Mandy, too," Ellen said.

Verna suppressed a sigh. Adam might not want his daughter to have her name shortened, but Amanda Rebecca seemed to have other plans.

"Actually," Verna said, giving the girl a knowing smile, "her father prefers to have her called by her full name, Amanda Rebecca."

"That is beautiful, too," Ellen said. "I've just made some apple cobbler if you two are hungry."

"I like cobbler!" Amanda Rebecca said.

"I thought you might, the minute I saw you." Ellen tapped her head with a twinkling smile. "Let me get you some."

Ellen bustled about getting some cobbler served into dishes, and Amanda Rebecca sidled up to the woodstove and held out her hands to warm them up.

"Congratulations on your wedding, my dear," Ellen said. "It happened so fast!"

"It was...arranged," Verna said, some warmth coming to her face.

"No shame in that," Ellen said. "We find our husbands how we find them, right? I was living right next door to Moe for years and years before we came to any agreements. Every couple is different, and I've heard that your Adam is very nice."

"He is," Verna said. "He's very kind, and I came home to a beautifully prepared house that we're renting. And he's raised a lovely daughter. I'm so happy."

That was what Amanda Rebecca needed to hear—that all was happy and well. And truly, Verna hoped it would be. It was a good first step that Adam had asked for her assistance in talking to the Stoltzfuses about their farm.

Ellen gave her a peculiar little smile, then turned to the girl with a plate of apple cobbler.

"Eat up, Amanda Rebecca," Ellen said. "I need you to watch out the window and count how many chickens come outside the coop. There are seven of them all together, and I have never seen all seven outside at once!"

"Seven?" Amanda Rebecca settled into a chair by the window and licked her lips as Ellen put the cobbler in front of her. She sat up on her knees to reach better and took a big bite.

Ellen nodded over to the sink, and Verna followed her. There were dishes to be done, but more importantly, there was privacy over there. Ellen started the water and squirted in some dish soap.

"It's new," Verna said quietly without prompting. "And I'm not sure I'm very good at being a wife yet..."

"Oh, you'll be just fine. His daughter already seems to like you quite a lot. That's the biggest hurdle."

That's what Verna had thought, too. But she remembered her promise to Adam. She would never reveal their bumps to people on the outside, and that included sweet Ellen

Stoltzfus, as well. With the water still running, Ellen began to wash the dishes.

"You're right, of course," Verna said. "And he does seem to like my cooking, which is a plus."

Verna accepted a bowl and picked up a tea towel to dry it. She looked over toward Amanda Rebecca, whose attention was in the cobbler at the moment.

"So you've stopped teaching your knitting class?" Ellen asked.

"Oh, no! I'm still teaching it."

"Even now?" Ellen looked over in surprise. "I hate to offer advice where it isn't asked for, but it might be better to quit it. I thought it was a wonderful addition to your life before marriage, but you have a home and family of your own now, and they'll need you."

But so did her students…in a different way, of course. And she needed them, too.

"There are four chickens outside!" Amanda Rebecca called. "One is a rooster!"

"Wonderful!" Ellen called back. "That rooster is new. I named him Absalom because he's noble and protective and beautiful, but he's awfully wily, too."

Verna chuckled at the little joke, grateful to let the previous comment pass by.

"I heard your husband has family connections out here," Ellen added, rinsing another dish and putting it into the sink.

"He does." Verna picked up the dish. "In fact, he wanted to meet you and Moe because Moe's old farm is the very land his great-grandparents lived on, a long time ago."

"Really?" Ellen's eyebrows rose. "That is certainly something."

"They're even buried there, somewhere," Verna said. "Adam and his brother Micah were working their father's farm in Oregon, and when Adam wanted to start looking for a wife, he was told that Redemption had some quality women, and it seemed like Gott's leading considering that his own family came from here."

"That does seem like the way Gott works," Ellen agreed with a nod as she turned her attention to a larger pot that required more scrubbing. "Who were they?"

"I'd have to ask him their names," Verna said. "There is so much I don't know, Ellen. But I do know that his family history here has given Adam a sense of belonging. But they were here long before your time, too."

"Yah, yah," Ellen agreed. "That was a long time ago. I wonder if your great-grandmother remembers them."

Verna straightened. "I wonder if she does…"

"It's amazing what the elderly can recall from years and years ago," Ellen said. "I mean, your great-grandmother is a little confused sometimes, but you could try asking her. She might remember the family."

"That's a good idea," Verna said. "I'll ask her about it the next time I have a chance." Verna sucked in a breath to stabilize herself. "But my husband was actually hoping to buy some land in these parts."

"There's an acreage up for sale in Bishop Joel's district," Ellen said.

"He was hoping…for something closer," Verna said.

"Ah, well, that's a difficulty. Mind, there might be others who know more about properties available than I do. I don't really keep up with all the ins and outs of it. I only know about the acreage because it was posted in *The Budget* newspaper."

"Has Moe's son decided to come work the land next door?" Verna asked.

"No, not yet. We're renting the pasture and crop fields out for the time being. I'm afraid the old house will start to molder away without a family in it soon, though."

"Have you considered…selling it?" Verna asked hopefully.

"Oh!" Ellen paused, then shrugged. "I mean,

we did discuss the possibility, but this involves Moe's children and their inheritance. That can be complicated. But Moe's the one to talk to about it. Although…" She looked thoughtful. "Moe's son Nathan has a greenhouse out in Ohio, and he's closer to his wife's family there. They have a disabled son who needs some extra help, and they've got the supports in place out there. The problem is, the family farm is here in Pennsylvania." She shook her head. "I've said before that selling the old place might be the way to pass the inheritance along without uprooting Nathan and his family."

Verna's heartbeat sped up. "Do you think Moe might consider it?"

"I'm not too sure," Ellen said. "He loves that land. His father worked that land, and he worked it every single day of his own life. The dirt under a man's boots can get into his blood, and my Moe is a gentle man, but when he gets his heart set on something, there's no budging him."

Still, Ellen could see the wisdom of selling that land, and maybe Moe would see it, too.

"It was just a thought," Verna said. "I only mentioned it because my husband was hoping, and… I want him to be happy."

"My dear, I'm sure you are everything he needs to be happy," Ellen said with a smile.

"A wife has a way of bringing comforts that a man didn't even know he needed."

"I hope so," Verna said.

Boots sounded on the step outside, and Verna and Ellen both turned to see the men come inside, their deep voices reverberating through the house as they chatted.

"I have brought Adam inside for your delicious cobbler, my dear," Moe said cheerily.

"Of course!" Ellen said, drying her hands. "Verna, let's let that pot soak and go sit with the men."

"There are six chickens in the yard now!" Amanda Rebecca announced excitedly from her seat by the window.

And Verna couldn't help but smile. This was her husband and daughter, and for the first time out together as a family, she felt that warm glow of pride—the acceptable kind of pride—in the precious people Gott had given her.

Ellen was right. The pot could wait. There was cobbler to enjoy, and visiting to do, and good impressions to make as a couple and as a little family.

Adam swallowed the last bite of sweet, tangy apple cobbler. Ellen was a kind old woman, and like most Amish ladies, she knew her way around a kitchen. She sat on a chair next to her husband once they were served, and Adam was a little embarrassed when he saw the tender looks pass between the old couple.

They were relatively newly married—he knew that much—but they also looked very much in love. It looked different on them than it had in Adam's first marriage. For the Stoltzfuses, they were calm and leaned ever so subtly toward each other.

Amanda Rebecca had some apple on her sleeve, and Verna leaned over and helped her clean it off so naturally that if someone didn't know she was a stepmother, they'd never guess it. He knew he was blessed in his new marriage, but he still wondered how the old couple had developed the bond they so obviously shared. It was calm, and deep, and exactly what Adam hoped for one day.

After eating apple cobbler and drinking some hot tea, Adam and Verna thanked Moe and Ellen for their hospitality and bundled up again to head out into the winter morning. It was actually closer to eleven at this point, and as Adam helped boost his wife and daughter up into the buggy, Verna's cotton dress brushing against his hand, he felt the wave of protectiveness he knew came with having a wife of his own.

Adam removed the blankets from the horses' backs, and the animals took a couple of prancing steps backward and forward, eager to get moving. He could see Verna's head bobbing around through the open door as she helped Amanda Rebecca to get settled in with her blankets over her legs and tucked underneath her. Then Adam finally settled in the buggy at Verna's side.

He always insisted upon meals first and treats later. He wanted fruits and vegetables eaten, and sweets limited in his home, but while he was chatting outside with Moe, the old man had said something that had made him think.

I like to be the one who brings a smile home at the end of the day, Moe had said. *That's all the family advice I have, I'm afraid.*

Adam didn't want to be the *daet* who always said no. Or who stopped the fun, or who denied treats. Not always. Sometimes, he wanted to be the fun one, too.

"Why don't we get a little treat on our way home?" Adam asked.

"A treat?" Amanda Rebecca piped up from the back. "What kind of treat? Do you mean a fresh apple? Because you said a fresh apple was a treat before."

Adam looked over his shoulder at his daughter's cautious expression. She would never forget that, would she? It had been almost a year ago now that he'd suggested an orchard fresh apple was a better treat than ice cream.

"How about some French fries?" he asked.

"Really, Daet?" She clasped her mittened hands under her chin.

"*Yah*. I think it would be good, don't you?"

"Yay! French fries!"

That was a yes from Amanda Rebecca, and he looked over at Verna, raising his eyebrows questioningly.

"*Yah*, that sounds very nice," Verna said with a smile. "I do enjoy French fries."

He was tired of disappointing these two. Let him be the one who brought some fun today, and who provided a treat. Besides, it felt like the right thing to do together as a family.

The ride into the town of Redemption didn't take very long. The town's Main Street shot all the way through from north to south and was lined with Amish businesses that catered to the tourists who frequented the area. But to the west side of town were the fast-food restaurants that the actual Amish people frequented most often.

A popular burger joint, Nelson's, had a drive-through, and in his younger days Adam used to take his buggy on through the drive-through window, much to the amusement of the Englishers. But he wasn't the same man now. He'd become more cautious, more serious, and he wouldn't pull up to the window this time. Besides, it was cold outside, and he imagined his daughter and his wife could use the warmth inside the restaurant.

"Did you talk to Ellen?" Adam asked as he reined the horses in at a buggy parking stall on the Amish row of the parking lot.

"I did," she said softly. "She says that—" She glanced over her shoulder, but Amanda Rebecca was bouncing on the seat in excitement, not listening at all. "She says that she thinks Moe selling is a good idea. I told her about your family's connection to the land, but she says that Moe's got a mighty strong tie to the land, too."

He nodded slowly. "Okay. That's good. It's a start. Moe invited me to come back one of these days and have a look around. I wanted to see if I could find some family graves. I know they're there. But after this amount of time…"

"You might find them," Verna said.

"I might." And the Stoltzfuses might sell the farm. Possibly. It would be difficult not to get his hopes up. "Would you like to come with me?"

"To look for the graves?" She stilled, her dark gaze locked on his face.

"Yah." He didn't sound as certain as he wanted to. It had occurred to him that having her there might be comforting—it might be appropriate, too. She was his wife, after all. This was her family now, too.

She nodded. "I would like that, Adam."

So would he.

"Ellen also suggested that I might ask my great-grandmother if she remembers your family at all."

"Would she?" he asked. "I mean…is she… Does she…" How did a man ask about an old woman's mental faculties after the age of one hundred?

"I don't know how much she'll remember, if anything," Verna replied. "But it's worth a try, isn't it?"

"Yah, I think it is," he agreed.

The fast-food restaurant was busier than he'd anticipated. It was very close to lunchtime, and the parking lot was full with mostly Englisher vehicles. There was only one other Amish buggy in the parking lot. A lineup of cars snaked out onto the road for the drive-through.

"Let's go inside," he said, and he held his hand out for Amanda Rebecca, who obediently took it and bounced along next to him.

His other hand was free, and he was tempted to take Verna's hand, too, but she had her hands clasped in front of her. Verna went ahead and she opened the door for him and Amanda Rebecca. The restaurant smelled of deep-fried deliciousness, and the murmur of chatting voices covered the clatter from the kitchen in a low, comforting hum.

There were three lines formed in front of tills, and they joined the nearest one. Verna looked ahead to the employee who was serving the family in front of them and she suddenly stilled. Adam shot her a curious look, but Verna didn't move. She simply pressed her lips together in a happy sort of way, her hands again clasped in front of her.

When they got to the front of the line, he noticed that the young woman serving them had hair dyed black on one side of her head and a bright, neon pink on the other side—all pulled into a short ponytail in the back and covered by a purple Nelson's Burgers baseball cap. She had several piercings going up the sides of her ears with big metal studs in them, and her face looked too white, like it had been painted. The short-sleeved shirt revealed tattoos on her arms—what looked like a snake and possibly a butterfly? It was hard to tell, and he didn't want to stare too much. The girl's appearance made him feel nervous—it was so different, so aggressive. He tugged his daughter behind him just a little bit. This was an example of the Englisher world out there, and he felt like this might be an example of why his *mamm* had converted to the Amish life. Amish teens would never dress like this.

"Miss Verna?" The girl's eyes widened, and suddenly she looked younger and a little more innocent.

"Blade!" A smile erupted over Verna's face, and then she looked nervously in Adam's direction.

Blade? What kind of a name was that? Verna knew this girl?

"Do you work here?" Verna stepped forward, lowering her voice a little more.

"Yeah, I started a few weeks ago," Blade said. "It's not bad. I get plenty of hours, and they don't make me take out my piercings." She smiled then. "I know you hate my piercings, Miss Verna."

"I didn't say that—" Verna started.

"You're too sweet to say it, but I can see it. But I like them."

"I know," Verna said. "It's okay."

But was it okay? Not to Adam. What kind of friendships had his wife developed?

"So is this—" Blade lowered her voice and looked shyly toward Adam, then back to Verna. "Is this *him*?"

"*Yah*, this is him. This is my husband, Adam, and my new daughter, Amanda Rebecca."

"He's cute." Blade grinned, and at least Verna had the sense to blush at that.

Cute. As if Adam cared what Englisher teens thought of his looks…but he might care about Verna's opinion.

"Nice to meet you," Blade said, giving Adam a frank look. Then she smiled down at Amanda Rebecca. "Your new mom is a really great lady. We all love her a lot."

"Who all?" Adam said in Pennsylvania Dutch.

Verna's gaze whipped toward him and she smiled nervously. "This is Blade. She's one my students learning knitting."

This girl—this strange-looking creature—was her *student*? Somehow he'd imagined teenagers with blue jeans and running shoes…not someone quite this shocking.

"Blade is learning very well," Verna went on a little breathily as if trying to fill the silence. "She's getting better every time we meet, and I'm very proud of her progress."

"I have a good teacher," Blade said with a grin. "But my knitting is awful." There was some murmuring behind them, and Blade's smile slipped. "Sorry, we'd better move this along. What can I get you?"

They ordered French fries and some drinks, and their food was piled onto a plastic tray.

"I'll see you Monday night, right?" Blade asked.

"If you aren't working, of course," Verna said.

"I won't be. It's court ordered, remember? I get those nights off, guaranteed." Blade's grin was wry and a little too old for her face.

Adam carried the tray and made his way as far from the service counter as he could, Verna and Amanda Rebecca following him. His pulse had sped up, and when he put the tray on a free table in the corner, he looked over at Verna. She wouldn't meet his gaze.

"That's your student?" he asked, his voice low.

"Yah."

"Court ordered? What does that mean?"

"It means that she's broken the law, and in order to meet the requirements of her punishment, she has to come to my class."

Adam wished she'd just quit. He wanted her to leave this in the past and never think of it again, but her gaze had turned bold as if she sensed what he was thinking. They'd agreed before the wedding that she'd continue teaching her class, among other things.

Instead, he opened a straw and poked it into the top of his daughter's small apple juice and set the drink in front of her.

He'd agreed to this, but his image of Verna's continual, reassuring presence in their home had started to dim. She'd fought for the right to continue teaching her class. She'd insisted that it was important and they needed her. And that young woman did seem to be very fond of his wife.

But why on earth would Verna put herself into such an environment? Why was it so important to her?

All questions for another time. His daughter was watching soberly.

"Let's pray," he said as he took a seat opposite Verna.

And they all silently bowed their heads. There was more to his wife than he'd previously thought, and maybe he shouldn't be surprised. People were always more complicated than they appeared…but why couldn't this time be different? Why couldn't Verna just be the simple, sweet Amish woman she appeared to be? Why couldn't her whole heart be centered upon their home the way the Amish idealized?

But deep down he knew the reason. Because they hadn't married for love—how could he expect her to pretend they had?

And Adam didn't know his wife half as well as he should. He'd have to rectify that. And maybe, when she trusted him more, she'd give this class up.

Chapter Six

The next day was Sunday. Verna always looked forward to Service Sunday, which came once over two weeks. That was the Sunday when they would gather together as a community to worship. The other Sundays were used to visit other communities, go to see family or just to rest at home. But that Sunday—the first Sunday after her wedding—they attended Service Sunday together as a family at Bishop Glick's farm.

Verna sat with Amanda Rebecca at her side on the women's side of the service, and she'd tried to keep her face from betraying any emotion at all when she looked at the sea of male faces across from them. Her *mamm* sat next to her, and her great-grandmother sat on the other side in a wheelchair with a thick blanket tucked around her legs. She dozed off and slept through most of the service.

After the service, Verna's parents had to take her great-grandmother home.

"Enjoy this," her *mamm* had said with a knowing smile. "This is the fun part! Spend time with your friends."

Everyone who stayed ate, and then Verna had the relief of visiting with her friends and answering their excited questions about her first few days of marriage. Was she happy? "Very." Was she finding keeping a house alone a lot more work than she thought? "Not really. I'm keeping up all right." Did her husband enjoy her cooking? "I think so, but it can be hard to tell because he's so polite." The women had chuckled and nodded knowingly at this, and she didn't really understand. Was being a stepmother difficult? "Not at all." In fact, the thing that she didn't say out loud was that Amanda Rebecca was the easiest part of this new marriage.

Verna had gone to bed that night exhausted, but relieved. Seeing her friends so happy for her new matrimonial state made her feel better. She'd settle in…wouldn't she?

Monday evening, Verna had a dinner of roast beef, boiled potatoes and a generous pile of steamed carrots ready to serve. She stood by the window, looking out into the dusky twilight, waiting for her husband's ride from work to appear at the top of the drive. The bare trees waved in a cold wind.

At the table, Amanda Rebecca sat with her meal in front of her. She'd eaten up the beef and one potato, but the carrots remained.

"Make sure you eat your carrots, honey," Verna said to Amanda Rebecca. "Your *daet* will want to know you did."

Amanda Rebecca stuffed a whole carrot spear into her mouth, and Verna smiled over at the little girl.

"Can I come with you tonight?" Amanda Rebecca asked, chewing, then swallowing.

"Well, your *daet* doesn't want you to, but if he isn't home in time, we might not have any other choice."

And her stomach sank at that thought. He really wouldn't want that, but she'd reminded him about her class tonight before he left for work.

"You could teach me, too!" Amanda Rebecca said. "I could be a student!"

"*Yah*, you could," Verna chuckled. "I'll get you started with your own knitting needles and some nice thick yarn."

If Amanda Rebecca could start learning to knit now, she could be quite skilled by the time she was a teenager. Verna couldn't remember learning to knit, it was so early, but her mother told her stories about her sitting with her own needles to learn as young as four years old.

Verna waited as long as she could, but when Adam didn't arrive home, she wrote a note and left it on the kitchen table next to a plate, cutlery and a cup.

Dear Adam,
I couldn't wait any longer. I'm so sorry.
I took Amanda Rebecca with me to my
class. Dinner is on the top of the oven,
and I do hope you enjoy it. I'll see you
this evening.
Verna

The note itself felt like it could use some endearment, and she'd even stopped before signing her name, wondering if she should add something. But what could she say? So she scrawled her name, left the piece of paper where Adam would see it right away, and she helped Amanda Rebecca bundle up for the ride into town.

When she arrived at the community center, she held Amanda Rebecca's hand as she led her through the hallway to the classroom. The AA meeting was in full swing, and the voices that filtered out into the hallway were encouraging.

"I just want Mike to know that he's not alone. I did the same thing when I first stopped drinking. It's not easy, but it's worth it..."

"Is that your class?" Amanda Rebecca whispered.

"No, that's another class of people who are working very hard to do better in their lives," Verna whispered back in Pennsylvania Dutch to keep her words more private still. "My class is this way."

She hadn't arrived as early as she usually did since she'd been waiting for Adam, and when she stepped into the classroom, some of the students had already arrived. Harry had moved the chairs into a circle already, and he sat in one of them, his legs spread and his arms crossed over his chest belligerently. He always looked like that, but Verna had learned that under his appearance of attitude was a lot of insecurity. Tia sat across from him, her knitting already out. She was looking at her scarf uncertainly.

"Good evening," Verna said. "I'm sorry I'm late."

"You aren't late," Harry muttered. "You just aren't early."

"This is an awful scarf," Tia said. "No one will want it."

"That isn't true at all," Verna said. "It's a beautiful scarf. It's your very first scarf, and when you look back on it, you'll remember all the work that went into it."

Tia and Harry looked over at her then, and they both froze for a moment when they spotted Amanda Rebecca standing next to her.

"Please meet my daughter," Verna said. "This is Amanda Rebecca. Amanda Rebecca, these are two of my students, Harry and Tia."

"Hey—" Jolene came into the classroom next. "You have a kid?"

"I do now," Verna said. "I recently got married, as you'll recall, and this is my new stepdaughter, but I'd rather call her my daughter. It's how I intend to love her."

"Nice." Jolene nodded a couple of times. "Hey, kid."

Amanda Rebecca stood in silence, staring at the strangers, and Verna's heart went out to her. This was nothing like anything the child had experienced before, and Verna put a reassuring hand on her shoulder.

"Amanda Rebecca wants to learn to knit, too," Verna said.

Abigail and Blade came into the room together, and there were introductions again—

although Blade remembered Amanda Rebecca from Nelson's Burgers. Then everyone got settled in their spots and pulled out their knitting.

"Okay, honey," Verna said, pulling another chair into the circle between her and Blade. "Come sit down, and I'm going to get you started, okay?"

Amanda Rebecca did as she was told, and for casting onto the needle—a nice, thick wooden one that would be easier for little hands—Verna had Amanda Rebecca just watch as Verna cast on ten stitches very slowly.

"I can't do that…" Amanda Rebecca whispered.

"It's okay," Verna said. "I just did it for you. Now, let's spread the yarn out and—do you see this loop here?"

For the next few minutes, Verna showed her daughter how to knit, moving the needles for her as Amanda Rebecca stared hard at the yarn.

"Where do I stab the needle next?" Verna asked.

Amanda Rebecca pointed hesitantly toward a loop of yarn, and Verna felt a thrill of pride.

"*Yah!* That's right!" Verna said.

"She's smart, huh?" Blade said.

Amanda Rebecca looked at Blade with a beaming smile. "I can learn it."

"Of course, you can learn it," Blade said. "You're just as smart as us. Maybe smarter— you never know."

"Smarter?" Amanda Rebecca sobered. "Really?"

"It's entirely likely," Blade replied with equal seriousness. "Now, pay attention, and your mom will show you how it's done."

Her mom…that was what Englishers called a *mamm*. She felt a smile tickle at her lips, and she was grateful for Blade's thoughtfulness there. For the next few minutes, she showed Amanda Rebecca how it was done, and then she let Amanda Rebecca do a few stitches on her own. They were hesitant and rather tight, but they were stitches.

"Now, I have to go check on the others," Verna said. "So you sit here and try by yourself."

Amanda Rebecca's face paled, but Verna had to see to her students. She got up and went around the outside of the circle, looking at their handiwork.

"Come here," Blade said to Amanda Rebecca. "Come sit with me and maybe we can do it together until Miss Verna comes back, okay?"

Amanda Rebecca smiled and sidled a little closer to Blade. She looked up at the leather jacket and touched a silver stud with the tip of her finger.

"You like that?" Blade asked.

Amanda Rebecca shook her head. "It's too sharp and scary looking."

Verna tried to smother a wince. *Kinner* were honest to a fault, but Blade hadn't seemed to take any offence.

"Yeah, that's what I was going for." Blade shot her a lopsided smile. "Come here. Let's knit."

Blade seemed quite patient, pointing to where the needle went and then helping guide when Amanda Rebecca missed the mark. Verna passed behind Harry, then Tia and Abigail. She paused at Abigail's knitting. She'd picked up yet another stitch, her scarf getting wider and wider as she knitted. She hesitated.

"You see, Abigail, the yarn got frayed here, and you turned it into two stitches instead of just one. If we back up a bit... May I?" Verna helped her eliminate the extra stitch and handed her scarf back carefully so as not to confuse her student. "There, now keep going. Very nicely done."

"I have to show this to my social worker

when it's finished," Abigail muttered. "I'm going to look like an idiot."

"No, you aren't," Verna said. "You'll look like a beginner. There's nothing wrong with showing how hard you worked on a brand-new skill. If you showed a perfect scarf, they'd never believe you, would they?"

"That's true," Tia said. "If we're going to get credit for this class, they have to believe we did the work ourselves."

"And mine is obviously done by a beginner," Blade added with a laugh.

"Sometimes we are new at things," Verna said. "Next door at the AA class, *yah*? They're new at not drinking. That's very hard to do if you've been used to alcohol for a long time. Here, we're new at knitting. But you'll be new at lots of other things in your lives. You might be new at a job—" she gave Blade a smile "—or new at making friends, or new at staying away from the wrong friends, or new at saying no to temptation… But one thing we Amish believe in is hard work. Hard work produces results, and practice makes perfect, or close enough to perfect. You're all doing very well at your knitting. I'm very proud of you."

"It helps to have a teacher," Harry said. "Who's gonna teach us the other stuff?"

"Oh, Harry, teachers are everywhere!" Verna said. "If you find someone who is doing something you wish you could do, you've found yourself a teacher. Maybe it's a man who is patient and never gives in to his temper. Well, he'll have some advice for you on how to do just that. Or maybe it's someone who's using a tool. He can teach you something about that job. It doesn't have to be in a classroom, does it?"

But as she spoke, she realized that she was preaching to herself just as much as she was preaching to her students. She was new at being married, and she was feeling nervous and uncertain, but she had friends who were married women. She even had one particular friend, Delia, who had been married for about fifteen years before her husband passed away. She might have time to pass along some wisdom to a new wife.

"What's that smile for?" Blade asked, looking up.

"I'm realizing that I'm no different than all of you. I can find more experienced women to give me some advice, too."

"About being married?" Abigail guessed.

The others all looked up and fixed her with those sharp, expectant stares. Sometimes she hated how perceptive these young people were. They never missed anything, did they?

"Maybe." Verna felt the heat hit her face. She looked quickly toward her daughter. This was not something to talk about in front of a child...or to anyone who wasn't a trusted confidant.

"Aw, you're embarrassing her," Blade said. "Miss Verna, I think you're doing just fine."

And Verna truly wished that Blade was right. But Verna wasn't doing just fine. She was slowly settling into a home with a man she didn't understand very well, and she slept in her own bedroom at night. That was no way to grow a family, and if anyone else knew, they'd certainly think she was failing as a wife.

But Delia just might understand...and she might have some tips on how to move this marriage into a closer relationship between her and her husband.

"We all start somewhere, is my point," Verna said. "And when we need advice, we need to ask for it."

Adam arrived home late. Someone had missed his shift at the dairy, and Adam had to cover for two extra hours until he could go home. When he came into the house, weary and hungry, everything was dark except for a soft, distant glow from inside the stove. He pulled off his gloves and coat, shivering in the cooling kitchen.

The first things he did were light the kerosene lantern and hang it over the kitchen table, then stoke the fire back up in the pot-bellied stove used for heat. The kitchen quickly began to heat up. He found the note on the table—he liked that she'd thought of him, but he also felt a wriggle of worry that Amanda Rebecca was at that class. An image of the pierced, tattooed student rose up in his mind. That was not the kind of influence he wanted on his Amish daughter.

His food was in the oven, and still warm. The beef was a little tough now, but he couldn't blame Verna for his lateness. He was sure it was a perfectly cooked roast two hours ago.

Adam bowed his head to thank Gott for the food, and for the wife who had cooked it, and then he quickly ate the meal. Even after being in the oven for two hours, the food was delicious. She seemed to know her way around a spice rack.

Afterward, he put his plate in the sink and headed upstairs to change out of his work clothes. He used to be accustomed to a quiet house when Amanda Rebecca was staying with her grandparents or spending time with cousins. It was his norm—just him and his memories. But in the short time since Verna had joined their family, this quiet began to feel odd and lonely.

Adam went into his bedroom. His bed was smoother than he was ever able to make it. She'd changed the sheets, and his bedding was clean and smelled of soft soap. He took off his work clothes and changed into clean broadfall pants and a fresh shirt. His room was still disorganized—various tools, some handkerchiefs and a broken straw hat he'd meant to repair on the top of his dresser, and on a rocking chair in the corner of the room sat a pile of extra blankets, some unmatched socks, a hardhat from a day job he'd taken when he first arrived and a few different pairs of work gloves in various states of "worn-out."

He should be neater. He put the handkerchiefs into a drawer, and then matched his socks and put them away. Then he looked at the rest and felt defeated already. He closed his door on the way out of his room and paused at Verna's. The door was open a crack and he nudged it open farther, the hinges creaking. He'd oil those hinges before she got home.

But first, he peeked into her room. The bed was made neatly, and hers seemed to have fresh sheets, too. The floor was swept and clean; her dresser top had the basket of yarn he'd bought her and nothing else. Her dresses hung neatly in her open closet, and her Bible lay on her bedside table next to a softly ticking clock.

What had she thought when she saw his bedroom, he wondered? Did she find him aggravating and impossible?

He noticed some knitting had been left on the seat of her own easy chair, angled toward the window. She was using the blue yarn he'd chosen for her, and a pot holder was taking shape. At least he thought it was a pot holder.

"She's using it…" he murmured aloud, and he smiled.

He'd really spent a lot of time and thought in choosing it all. It was nice to have his attempt at a gift appreciated.

Adam headed back to his own bedroom and rooted around in a cardboard box of tools and some grease and shoe polishes. He came up with a can of WD-40 and a rag, and he went back over to her door. For the next couple of minutes, he sprayed lubricant into the hinges and then swung the door open and shut, making the hallways smell faintly of the chemicals that greased the hinge. When the door moved smoothly and silently, he wiped all the hinges down with the rag.

There. Would she notice? He hoped so.

Outside, he heard the clop of the horse's hooves, and he tossed the rag into the "laundry corner" of his bedroom where he'd left his soiled work clothes, then pulled the door shut. That was a problem for another day. Right now, he'd go outside and take care of the horse and unhitch the buggy. He was determined that as long as he was present, his wife and daughter would never have to do that particular chore.

Adam trotted down the stairs feeling cheerier already that they were back. He plunged his feet into his boots and grabbed his coat and a scarf. The kitchen was already nice and warm, the stove burning merrily, the stove pipe ticking with heat. He lit another kerosene lantern and headed out into the cold evening.

Verna was just descending from the buggy as he strode up. Amanda Rebecca held two large knitting needles with a few rows of knitting on it in front of her, her eyes glowing.

"Daet, I knitted this!" She thrust the needles toward him proudly. "I knitted it!"

There were a couple of inches worth of knitting on the needles, and he was surprised. Could his daughter knit now? Was she really that advanced? Could he tell the other farm hands at his job that his young daughter was well and truly knitting?

"With help?" He looked over at Verna, then lifted his daughter out of the buggy and set her on the ground.

"A little bit," Verna said. "But she did at least one row by herself with no help. I was very impressed with her."

"Blade says I'm a good knitter!" Amanda Rebecca said, spinning in a circle. "And Tia says I'm better at knitting than all of them! And they're teenagers!"

"Did they?" he asked, watching as Amanda Rebecca danced around in the trodden snow.

"*Yah*! And I know where to stab the needle now. And I can loop the yarn and then you tug it back through the hole, and Harry says that it's like catching a cat! *Mee-ow!*" Amanda Rebecca mimicked. "Right back through the hole!"

"You'd never pull a cat through a hole!" he said. "You should never treat an animal that way."

"A joke…" Verna's voice was low, but more insistent. "It was just to make her laugh. And it helped her to find it fun. That's all. No one would mistreat a cat."

He rubbed his gloved hand over his bearded chin. "Is this wise, Verna?"

"It was just a joke—"

"I mean, bringing her to the class," he clarified.

"You weren't home, Adam," she said. "And they were all very kind to her. It was knitting—nothing else."

"That girl from Nelson's," he said. "I don't like Amanda Rebecca to spend time with her. She's everything we want our daughter to avoid."

"She's also got a good heart," Verna said softly. "And while she's made plenty of mistakes, she's a very earnest girl. She comes across as brittle and tough, but under that she's really very sweet."

Adam looked down at his bright-eyed daughter. He couldn't say too much in front of her.

"There are influences we'd rather avoid," he said meaningfully.

"*Yah*, I do agree, Adam," Verna said.

"I don't want Amanda Rebecca around her."

"It's hard to avoid in a knitting circle. She was very patient with Amanda Rebecca. She helped teach her."

So that terrifyingly different teenager had been teaching Amanda Rebecca. He shut his eyes for a moment trying to beat back the frustration rising inside of him.

"Amanda Rebecca, go inside and get warm," Adam said.

"Now?" his daughter asked.

"*Yah*, now. Go on. The kitchen is nice and toasty. Go get yourself warmed up."

Amanda Rebecca looked at him from the corner of her eye, then headed off toward the house. He hoped his aggravation wouldn't show on his face, but from the wary look Verna gave him—one rather similar to the look on his daughter's face—he was pretty sure he'd failed there. He was the fun-ruining *daet* again.

"She's young and impressionable," Adam said. "And if she thinks that girls with tattoos and dyed hair and piercings are *wunderbar*, then what will hold her to our faith? If she thinks that life outside of our faith is just fine—no problems with it—why live a harder life here with us?"

"Those *kinner* have made very big mistakes," Verna said. "And we will have to explain that to her, but right now, it would only ruin her experience of learning to knit. I don't want her to be frightened of them."

"But if that fuller explanation waits too long," Adam said, "she'll glorify those teenagers in her mind. She'll wish to be like them."

"No…"

"She will." He shook his head. His little brother had, until the Englisher boys had turned on him. "They aren't trustworthy, Verna."

"Actually, they have been honest with me—"

"Verna, I've seen Englisher *kinner*. I've seen what they can do. Do they have hearts? Of course! They feel awful after having caused damage. But the damage is still there! And this is *my* daughter! If anything happened to her…"

Verna blinked at him, and tears rose in her dark eyes. Her eyelashes moistened, but she blinked back the tears. He felt a wave of regret. He'd done it now—he'd hurt her.

"She's yours," she said, her voice tight.

"She's *ours*," he amended. "I don't mean that you aren't her—"

"*Step*mother." Her chin trembled. "I haven't been calling her my stepdaughter, though. Because I wasn't going to love her like a stepdaughter. I wanted to love her like my very own. But she's your daughter. Not mine. I'm clear on that."

That she'd wanted to love Amanda Rebecca

like her own was utterly beautiful—the very heart he'd prayed for when he asked Gott to lead him to the right wife.

"Verna…"

Verna turned toward the horse and started with the buckles. She pulled off her gloves, and her fingers were red with cold.

"Verna, I'll do that. That's men's work."

"Danke." She released the buckle, but her voice was tight. He had to explain himself. He wasn't the tyrant. He really wasn't!

"I don't want Amanda Rebecca to be drawn to that life," he said. "I don't want her to get hurt, or taken away from our faith."

"Neither do I, Adam."

Of course…but the best of intentions didn't always protect a child. He knew that from experience. Still, standing outside in the cold with his wife near tears—this wasn't right, either.

"I apologize if I raised my voice or…was harsh," he said.

"It's okay. I understand."

Perfectly polite and sweet, but she didn't really understand him. On the surface perhaps, but the depth of his fear…that wasn't something she felt, too.

"Go on in and get warm," he said gruffly. "You look frozen through."

Verna headed toward the house, and he looked over his shoulder, watching her retreating form. Then he turned back to the horse.

That hadn't gone the way he'd hoped. He'd wanted Verna to see it his way, to see why he was afraid for his daughter, and share in that alarm. He wanted to feel that they were united on this, but they were not.

And while Amanda Rebecca was indeed their daughter to raise together, she was biologically his. Would a stepmother—even one with as big a heart as Verna's—love her quite the same?

Chapter Seven

The next morning, after Adam had gone to work and the kitchen was clean, Verna hitched up the buggy and drove with Amanda Rebecca down the back roads toward the Swarey Flower Farm. Delia and her four sons ran the farm together, and they grew flowers for florists and other decorating professionals who needed fresh blooms for display.

The day was warm, rising up above freezing so that the bright sunlight melted the last of the snow and ice from the roads and gleamed off the horse's glossy coat. Birds twittered from the fence wires, hopping down into the seeded grasses below that grew up past the snow. Another buggy passed them going the other direction, and Verna waved at the old man who was driving. He was one of her father's good friends.

"They have flowers in wintertime?" Amanda Rebecca had asked this question several times already, completely shocked by the possibility.

"*Yah.* They have warm greenhouses where they grow them in pots," Verna said. "You'll see. It's very pretty. Haven't you seen flowers in the supermarket?"

She nodded.

"Well, that's where they come from—flower farms like Delia's."

"Wow…" the girl whispered.

This little piece of information gave Amanda Rebecca something to ruminate on for the last stretch before they reached Delia's farm. When Verna pulled into the drive, she spotted Delia's oldest son, Ezekiel, pulling a hose behind him as he headed into a greenhouse. He seemed to hear the horse, because he turned and shaded his eyes.

Delia appeared in the doorway of the greenhouse, a winter coat on and a big gray apron on top of both coat and dress.

"Hello!" Delia called, waving. Verna waved back, and Delia came in their direction.

"Do you see those long, round buildings?" Verna pointed for her daughter's benefit. "That's where they grow the flowers. They get enough sunlight through the roof, and they stay warm inside from those solar panels on top."

"And there's flowers inside?"

"There are flowers inside." She cast the girl a smile.

Verna hopped down from the buggy and Amanda Rebecca hopped down next to her without any help this time. Delia's youngest son, Moses, came out of the stable with something in his arms, and he waved at Verna, too. Delia had raised some good *kinner*, and there might come a time when she came to Delia for a little parenting advice, too.

"How are you?" Delia said, breathing briskly when she reached them.

"I'm doing very well," Verna said, then she hugged her friend. "I want you to meet my new daughter. This is Amanda Rebecca."

"Hello, Amanda," Delia said with a broad smile. "It's so very nice to meet you. I'm so glad you came to visit."

Moses came up to them as they reached the step, and Amanda Rebecca spotted what the boy was holding before Verna did.

"A kitten!" she squealed. "Do you have kittens?"

"*Yah*. There's six more in the stable." Moses straightened his shoulders a little bit.

"Can I go see them?" Amanda Rebecca pleaded.

"Are there horses inside today?" Verna asked.

"No, they're all outside in the pasture," Moses said.

"Well, then, I don't see why not," Verna said. "You listen to Moses, Amanda Rebecca. He knows the rules in the stable."

Moses was eleven years old and certainly old enough to keep an eye on her, so long as she listened.

"I will!" Amanda Rebecca reached to pet the little ball of fur in Moses's hands, and he passed the kitten over to her keeping.

"You can carry him, if you want," Moses said. "Come on. I'll show you the others, too."

"Can you show me the flowers, too?" Amanda Rebecca asked as they tramped away together. Verna didn't hear the reply, but Amanda Rebecca walked with her head down over the kitten in her arms.

"She's very sweet," Delia said. "I prayed for a girl, but Gott gave me four boys. Gott knows what we need most, and I don't know how I'd run this place without my boys to help. But you are blessed with a sweet little girl, Verna."

Verna shot her friend a smile. She knew she could count on Delia to be happy for her.

"It's a good thing she's distracted with the kittens, because I wanted to talk to you, woman to woman," Verna said.

"Oh?" Delia sobered. "Well, we might not have much time before they come back, so let's get inside and I'll put the tea on."

Verna followed her friend inside the house. The kitchen was far from clean. A pile of dishes sat on the counter, boys' sweaters were hung over the backs of chairs and there was a little inexplicable pile of pinecones on the corner of the table.

"Don't mind the mess," Delia said. "We'll all work at cleaning it up together this evening."

She took off her apron and coat and hung them both up, then stepped out of her boots. Verna followed her example, and Delia put a kettle on the stove and bent down to stoke up the flames and add more wood.

Verna moved over to the warm stove and held out her hands.

"Now…" Delia said. "How can I help?"

Verna smiled uncomfortably, and she felt her cheeks warm. "It's about marriage."

"Ah."

"My problem is… I don't know how to do

this. I saw my parents' marriage, of course. Mamm cooked and cleaned and knew what Daet liked. Daet was considerate and kind and worked hard. But they shared a connection that was special."

Delia nodded. "*Yah*, that's a beautiful thing."

"I don't—" Verna licked her lips. "I don't know him, Delia. And I had hoped that maybe just by being married, by having said those vows, that Gott would give us that connection, but so far, it hasn't happened."

"Ah."

"I don't know why!" Verna added. "You don't know how much I've prayed!"

"Oh, Verna, some things are spiritual, and some are just logical," Delia said. "Every new marriage has its awkwardness. When I married Zeke, I had some awkward times, too. And I knew him since I was a young girl, and he courted me for three years."

"What hope have I got then?" Verna asked miserably.

"All sorts of hope," Delia replied. "There are methods, you see. Ways to soften things between a couple."

"Like what?" she asked.

"Well, first of all, there's food." Delia shrugged. "You cook delicious meals, have pies waiting for him when he gets in from the stable and fry his bacon to the perfect crispiness that he loves, and suddenly you find him looking at you in a whole new way."

"Food."

"*Yah*. Men like their comforts, and they'll be walking a little faster to get inside if they know you're waiting with something delicious for them."

"Okay... I've been doing that already, though."

"Do you listen to him when he talks?" Delia asked.

"When he talks I listen, but he doesn't talk too much," she replied. "And mostly we've been disagreeing on subjects."

"You could try agreeing with him."

"But it's about things that matter—like my knitting class. I know he doesn't like me teaching it, but I can't give it up. Those Englisher *kinner* need me, and I need to be needed, you know?"

"Aren't you needed at home?"

"*Yah*, but..." Verna smoothed her hands down her dress. How to explain it all? How to tell that without a husband who'd fallen in love with her, she needed somewhere else to be needed, too?

"Okay, okay," Delia said soothingly, not

seeming to require more. "There's bound to be conversations like those, too, in your first year of marriage. There is some negotiation that happens, and some coming to terms with your spouse's ways."

"Is there anything else I might try?"

Please, let there be something!

"Of course!" Delia said. "And this is the most important tool a woman has in her marriage. This is what makes all the difference."

"Yah?" She leaned forward.

"Flirting."

Verna blinked. "What now?"

"Flirting. And I'm completely serious," Delia said. "This is very important. There is no other man on this green Earth that you are permitted to flirt with. Besides, it makes your husband feel special. There is no one else who he can *allow* to flirt with him, either, is there?"

"But…how?"

"You laugh at his jokes. Look him in the eye and smile. Touch his arm when you talk to him. Do you remember having a wild crush on some boy as a teenager?"

"Of course, but—"

"Well, think about the sorts of ways you would have flirted back then. It translates to womanhood. Make him feel like the most important man in the world. Flirt with him." Delia shot her a smile. "I think you'll do just fine."

She imagined doing just that with her stern new husband and winced.

"I'm not sure he'd like it," she admitted.

"Verna, every man likes it," Delia said. "It might surprise him, but it'll stay with him. Flirt with your husband. That is the secret to a long and happy union. I promise you that. I know from experience."

And Delia had had a very happy marriage to Zeke... This was why Verna had come to her friend—for some practical advice to bring home and put into practice.

But flirting... She'd never really tried to flirt before. She'd tended to look ridiculous when she'd tried as a teenager, and her single status all the way up until age thirty should be proof enough of the lack of her own flirting skills.

"You don't need to worry, though," Delia said. "You have your community here to help you on your way. You aren't alone in this."

"I know," Verna said.

"When I first married Zeke, I moved out here to be with him," Delia said. "It was hard, those first few years. I was so lonely for my sisters and my friends, and..." She sighed. "It was hard. Very hard. But couples figure these things out, and Zeke and I were no different. So I'm not complaining, not really. I suppose what I'm trying to say is that you have less to worry about. You have your family and friends. It really does help."

Verna was certain that it would. Delia wasn't the only woman to have moved to their community when she got married. There had been others, and not every story was so happily recalled. Verna had seen young wives sobbing behind the outhouse at Service Sunday, thinking no one could see them… Loneliness made everything worse, and she could only thank Gott that her husband promised that they'd stay in Redemption.

Moses and Amanda Rebecca came tramping up the steps, and Verna turned to see both children standing with their boots still on their feet on the kitchen floor. Amanda Rebecca held a fluffy little ball of white and gray fur, and her eyes were shining.

"Mamm, may I have a kitten?" Amanda Rebecca pleaded. "May I?"

She'd called her Mamm…spontaneously! Verna's heart tumbled with happiness, then sank. Adam had made it clear who had the final say with their daughter, and while he'd tried to take it back, she knew how he felt.

"I think we'd better talk to your *daet* about that," Verna said.

"But if Daet says it's okay, can I?" Amanda Rebecca's lips parted, and she stood there, hope shining in her eyes.

"Let me see the kitten," Verna said instead, and Amanda Rebecca came tramping over to where Verna stood and held out the tiny thing.

"Oh, the floor," Verna said to Delia. "I'm sorry. I'll mop for you."

"Nonsense," Delia said with a laugh. "Finding a home for a kitten is recompense enough if you end up taking one home with you."

The kitten was tiny and soft, and it mewed so plaintively that Verna's heart went out to it. A little more company in the house would be nice during the day, and she knew Amanda Rebecca would love a pet to dote on.

She looked up at Delia, and her friend crossed her arms over her chest.

"I came for some friendly advice, not a kitten," Verna said with a laugh.

"You can have both," Delia replied. "And as for the advice, just try it. I think you'll be pleasantly surprised."

Delia would know, wouldn't she? If Adam agreed, she'd come back for this kitten, and even if she looked completely ridiculous, she would attempt to flirt.

* * *

Adam got home that evening at the proper time. He could smell the cabbage rolls as soon as he opened the door. He'd been thinking about dinner ever since four o'clock when he was helping with the final milking, hooking up the cows to the milking machine and thinking that it had been quite some time since lunch.

He'd been getting some good-natured teasing from the Englisher men he worked with when he told them he'd gotten married. They'd been talking about all the good food he'd be getting, and they weren't wrong. So far, Verna's cooking was beyond compare. Normally when a couple courted, a woman would cook many good meals for her man before the big day. But they'd gotten married so quickly that he honestly hadn't been sure what kind of cooking he'd be in for.

Adam shut the door and pulled off his boots.

Amanda Rebecca came skipping up to the door while he hung his coat on the hook next to Verna's shawl. His daughter's hair hung in a pale blonde braid down her back, and she wore a small knitted sweater—it looked new. Had Verna made it?

"Hello, Amanda Rebecca," he said with a smile.

"Hello, Daet! We're having cabbage rolls."

"My favorite." He hadn't had good cabbage rolls since the last wedding he'd attended in Oregon, and they'd been part of the wedding dinner.

"And I helped make them. I mashed a big bowl of meat with my fingers."

"With clean fingers," Verna added, a sparkle in her eye.

"*Yah*, I washed my hands very well, and then I mashed it up." She held up her fingers in demonstration.

He met Verna's gaze. She really was a good stepmother. She was including Amanda Rebecca in the cooking—Amanda Rebecca would learn that way. By the time she was a teenager, she'd be an excellent baker and cook just because she would have helped since she was small.

Verna crossed the kitchen. "Are cabbage rolls really your favorite?"

"*Yah*, I love cabbage rolls."

She smiled, fixing him with her bright gaze. "I didn't know. That's good that I had a hankering for them today, then."

"Amanda Rebecca didn't say?" he asked.

"Amanda Rebecca assured me that you like pie," she said with a small smile.

"I wanted pie," Amanda Rebecca said. "And you do like pie, Daet."

Where had this outspoken little girl come from? He cocked his head to one side and regarded his daughter with a smile tickling his lips. She was certainly more energetic now.

"You could have told me, you know," Verna said.

"I don't want to put you out," he said. The last thing he wanted was to inconvenience her and make her cook things that he liked. What about foods that she liked? What about foods that comforted *her*? And she wasn't a restaurant. He wouldn't put in orders for his meals. She was a wife who cooked for her family, and he would be grateful for the food put in front of him.

Verna laughed then, a bright, cheerful laugh, and he stared at her, stunned. Had he said something funny? Her laughter stopped, and she cleared her throat.

"Was that funny?" he asked uncertainly.

"No…not really." Her faced grew red. "I'm sorry."

"Don't be sorry for being happy," he said.

"I'm not, I—" She shook her head. "It's okay. Never mind. I just mean, if you tell anyone the food you like, it should be your wife, *yah*?"

"Oh...*yah.*"

She stood there, her eyebrows raised, watching him.

"I really do like cabbage rolls," he said slowly, not too sure what else to say.

She sighed, deflating a little bit.

"They smell wonderful," he added. Would that help?

"That's good to know," Verna replied with a nod. "I hope you like these. They're my great-grandmother's recipe, but I've made a few tweaks to them."

Verna headed back to the stove and put on some oven mitts. She opened the oven door and pulled out a big roasting pan, hoisting it up to the stove top. Then she closed the oven and lifted the lid. He joined her at the stove and looked down into the roasting pan. A layer of cabbage leaves covered the top, the leaves a little blackened. Verna used tongs to pull those away, and underneath was a neat layer of small rolls wrapped tightly in cooked cabbage leaves, tomato sauce bubbling around them. His stomach rumbled.

"What do you do differently with your cabbage rolls?" he asked her.

"That's a secret." She lifted one finger, and then cocked her head to one side. "Well, I suppose I can tell *you,* can't I?"

Her voice sounded rather coy. What had gotten into her today? His sober, almost regal wife was acting like a schoolgirl. He eyed her uncertainly.

"I imagine you could," he said cautiously.

"Oh, you…" She laughed again and swatted his hand gently. He instinctively pulled his hand away.

Really—what was happening here? Had she gone out today and completely lost her mind? He'd been getting comfortable with Verna over the last week, and today she was like a completely different woman.

"I add some pickled spinach and rice to the meat filling," she said, growing more serious. "It's quite tasty, I've been told."

She took a small plate from the counter and dished up a single cabbage roll, then passed it to him with a fork. It was dripping with tomato sauce and smelled wonderful.

"Try one." Verna's gaze locked on his face, and he glanced up at her a little uncertainly. Her direct, gray gaze was daunting.

"Okay…" He cut into the roll with the side of his fork and sampled some of the filling. The meat was tender and flavorful, and the rice and pickled spinach melded together with the tomato sauce. "Mmm. This is very good. Wow."

These were the best cabbage rolls he'd ever tasted, actually. They trumped his own mother's—not that he'd ever be able to admit that in his mother's presence.

"Danke." Verna's cheek pinked. "I do my best."

She put a hand on his arm, and he stopped chewing. The blush in her cheeks deepened, and she pulled her hand quickly back. She snatched the plate from his hand, three quarters of a cabbage roll still on it, and walked briskly to the counter. He held his fork aloft, wondering if he could ask for his plate back.

"Daet?" Amanda Rebecca stood in front of him, big blue eyes fixed on his face. "Can I have a kitten?"

Verna stood with her back to him, rigid, straight. She picked up a pile of three dinner plates and brought them to the table. He'd never seen a woman quite so forward as Verna was being this evening. And it wasn't that he didn't like it… It just confused him. Where was it coming from?

"Daet, can I have a kitten?" Amanda Rebecca repeated.

"A…what?" He could feel the spot on his bicep where Verna's fingers had lingered.

"We saw people today who have seven kittens," his daughter said, "and I can have one if you let me!" Amanda Rebecca stood up on the tips of her toes, her eyes opened as far as they could possibly open.

"A kitten?" He looked down at his daughter with a frown, tuning in to what she was saying.

"*Yah!* A kitten! There is one that is gray and white, and she's my favorite. I'd name her Smokey. And I'd take very good care of her."

"If it's a girl, we'd have to get the cat spayed, and that's expensive," he said.

"Oh…" Amanda Rebecca dropped down off her tiptoes.

"And there's the cleaning up after the cat, too. Is it to be a stable cat?"

"No, it would be inside with me," Amanda Rebecca said. "I will cuddle it and sleep with it."

"Then there would be a litter box to be cleaned," he said.

"I can do that!"

"I'm not sure you can, Amanda Rebecca. That's not a job for a little girl your age. It's… a more grown-up job."

And if he didn't want to bother Verna with his dinner requests, then he certainly didn't want to increase her workload by adding in a pet if she didn't want one. And yet, this was the happiest he'd seen his daughter in a long time. With Verna, it was like Amanda Rebecca was blossoming into a more joyful child.

"Well… I'll grow!" Amanda Rebecca said. "I'll get bigger!"

"What did your *mamm* say?" he asked, looking over at Verna. If Verna didn't want a cat, he would end this right now.

"She said we had to ask you," Amanda Rebecca said.

He caught Verna's eye, wondering where she stood with this, and she just shrugged. "You're the final say with her."

Right. The argument they'd had. He'd spoken too quickly, and now those words were going to haunt him, weren't they? But he'd been thinking that over lately, too, and he knew that if Amanda Rebecca was going to be *their* child, and if he wanted her to be no different than any other babies that might come in the future, then he'd have to let Verna have the rights and power of a mother.

"Well…" Adam said slowly. "I don't think I'm the one who should make that decision. I'm not home all day, and Verna, you're the one who runs this house and you have a sense of what Amanda Rebecca can handle. I will defer to you in this. It's your decision."

The room silenced, and all that he could

hear was the steady tick of the heat in the stovepipe.

"Really, Adam?" Verna's voice was soft.

"Yah." He wasn't sure what else to say—at least in front of his daughter.

Amanda Rebecca turned those wide, pleading eyes on Verna, and he wondered if Amanda Rebecca softened Verna as efficiently as she softened him.

"If it's truly up to me, then I think that a kitten would be a nice addition to our home," Verna said. "I saw the kittens, Adam. They're adorable."

"Yay!" Amanda Rebecca erupted in a joyful spin. "A kitten of my very own! Thank you, Daet! Thank you, Mamm!"

Verna smiled and turned toward the kitchen. She came back with a large bowl of steaming boiled potatoes and put it on a knitted pot holder on the center of the table. Next came a bowl of boiled beets, then some squash. Lastly, she brought the big pan of cabbage rolls and set them right in front of Adam's plate.

"Amanda Rebecca, go and wash your hands upstairs," Adam said.

Still overjoyed about the kitten, Amanda Rebecca bounded up the stairs, leaving him and Verna alone for some precious few minutes.

"Verna, what's going on?" he asked softly, fixing her with a meaningful look.

"Do you mean the kitten?" Her cheeks pinked again.

"I mean…" How was he supposed to explain this without hurting her feelings? Was this what Verna was like when she was happy, perhaps? "I mean you are acting—I mean, you are seeming…" But there was no polite way to say she was acting completely differently than he'd ever seen her before.

"I know what you mean." She rubbed her hands over her face. "I'm embarrassed."

"Why?" He leaned forward.

"I was given some marriage advice today." She peeked over the top of her fingers, then lowered her hands. "My friend said that I should flirt with you."

"Flirt?" He blinked at her. "Is that what all this was? Flirting?"

"I didn't say I was any good at it," she said defensively. "There's a reason I was single so long."

Flirting… Some well-meaning woman had sat his wife down and suggested that she flirt with him? Is this what women talked about when they were alone?

Adam chuckled. "It just surprised me."

"I'm sorry. It was silly. I'll stop it," she said, shaking her head.

She was embarrassed now, and he felt bad about that. He didn't want her to feel bad. She'd been doing it for *him*—trying out some advice to make him happy. It was touching, really.

"Well, now… I didn't say *that*," he countered.

"No? Do you…like it?"

What he liked was seeing her happy. And he had liked the feeling of her hand on his arm, too, he had to admit. And if he'd actually said something funny, it would be nice to hear her laugh.

"My friend said that there's no one else I can flirt with, and she pointed out that there's no one else you can allow to flirt with you, either." Verna licked her lips. "And she said that flirtation makes for a happy marriage."

"I do want us to be happy." Adam felt some warmth on his own cheeks. "I'm not opposed to advice on a happy marriage. Now that I know what is happening, I won't be so surprised."

"Okay." She dropped her gaze.

"If you wanted to flirt again… I would be okay with it," he added.

"Now?" She blinked at him. "Because I'm not sure I can right now. I'll feel silly."

"Then maybe not now," he said. "But when you'd like to."

"Okay." She met his gaze then, and his heart gave a little flip. She really was a beautiful woman.

Amanda Rebecca came back down the stairs and slid onto her booster seat.

"Let's pray," Adam said.

He bowed his head for silent prayer—thankful for the food, and for his daughter, and for his wife. And then, as he cleared his throat to show that the prayer was over, another thought struck him.

Did this mean he was going to have to flirt back? Because he knew as much about flirting as she did!

Chapter Eight

The next morning after Adam went to work, Verna took Amanda Rebecca in the buggy back to Delia's flower farm. Amanda Rebecca bounced on the seat next to her the entire drive, jiggling and swinging her legs in excitement.

"I hope the gray kitten hasn't been taken," Amanda Rebecca said. "I hope no one else wanted her!"

"I think the chances of the gray kitten still being there are very high, honey," Verna chuckled.

Farms were forever finding themselves with litters of kittens they weren't expecting, and Delia would have a challenge finding homes for that newest litter. Maybe a few of them would be good mousers. But she'd have to make sure she got the female cats spayed, or else she'd have another surprise litter, no doubt.

When Verna pulled onto Delia's property, young Moses was the one who met them.

"Hi, Mandy!" he said. So it seemed that her little nickname was already flourishing over here, too. Verna couldn't bring herself to say anything, especially since Amanda Rebecca had made a friend. That could be difficult enough sometimes without adults meddling in the middle.

"Hi!" Amanda Rebecca hopped down. "I get a kitten, Moses!"

"Really?" Moses looked up at Verna. "She can have one?"

"Do you still have the gray one?" Amanda Rebecca asked. "The gray one with the white nose?"

"Yah…we've still got all of them," Moses said with a laugh. "You want to come find your kitten?"

Delia emerged from the house then and waved at Verna.

"Come inside, Verna!" she called. "Have you returned for a kitten?"

"*Yah!* They're going to choose it now." Verna draped a blanket over the horse's back and put a feed bucket within reach for him.

Then she headed over to the house where her friend was waiting.

"That'll bring me down to six kittens to find homes for," Delia chuckled as she held the door for Verna. "Come in. I'm just finishing up some baking. I can't put off the bread any longer."

The house smelled of yeasty rising dough, and the stove pumped heat out into the room.

"Are you sure you don't want two kittens?" Delia asked with a twinkle. "Or three?"

"No, no!" Verna laughed. "One is all we can handle now, and I don't want to go back to Adam asking for more cats. He's been patient enough."

"How are things going?" Delia asked as she turned a bowl of dough out onto the countertop.

"Well… I tried to flirt," Verna said with an embarrassed laugh. "I didn't make you proud, Delia. I'm afraid I confused him more than anything."

"Oh, no," Delia chuckled. "It's to your credit that you have no practice at it, Verna."

"Except, now that I'm married, I need to learn how to do some of these things rather quickly."

"I know…" Delia cast her an understanding smile. "That's the way it is, isn't it? But the beautiful thing about a marriage is that you have nothing but time. You have the rest of your life."

"*Yah*. And he did say he didn't mind if I flirted a little." Verna winced. "That was after I explained what I was doing... He didn't know."

"That sounds like a good start to me," Delia said. "Really, it's a matter of figuring him out, you know? I can give all the advice of what worked with Zeke, but...that was our relationship. And that was Zeke."

Delia's eyes misted, and she turned her attention to kneading the dough.

"You miss him," Verna said.

"I will always miss him," Delia said. "He was the best husband a woman could ask for. He was kind, attentive, funny, hardworking... and just the best father for my boys." She looked up at Verna, her hands still working the floury dough. "Treasure him. Don't ever take him for granted. Enjoy his male ways around the house, because now I miss all those things that used to bother me. I used to hate how he'd leave his socks on the bedroom floor, or how I'd find the bar of soap in the bathroom all covered in gray suds from him washing his hands... I even miss him being grumpy before dinner because he was hungry. So treasure that man."

Adam was polite and kind...there was no question of that. But he was rather distant, too.

"I'm not sure he'll let me," Verna said softly.

"Why do you say that?" Delia asked.

"Because he's very serious," Verna said. "And he likes things a certain way. And he..." He held her at arm's length. But that was going to sound like complaining, and it was awfully close to what Adam's first wife had done. She wouldn't hurt him that way. "Really, I'm just scared of looking silly. I'll get over it. Don't worry."

"You've only been married a week!" Delia said, flopping the dough back into the bowl and covering it again with a cloth.

"A week and a day," Verna chuckled. "I got married last Tuesday, and today is Wednesday."

"A week and a day," Delia said with a small smile. "It's not very long. I think you're doing very well. Your stepdaughter seems to love you, and from the outside, you look completely happy and in control."

At least she was making a good impression. She didn't feel nearly as confident as that. But she was going to do something else today—something just for Adam.

"I'm going to sit down with my great-grandmother today and ask her if she remembers anything about Adam's family from years ago," Verna said. "Adam's grandfather lived here in this area, and I wanted to see if Sarah remembered anything from their time here."

Verna's great-grandmother was the oldest member of their community, after all.

"That's a wonderful idea!" Delia brightened. "You see? You're doing just fine. You're getting to know your husband."

"I hope so!" But Verna smiled all the same. "I think it might help him to feel more connected here. I have all my friends and family, and he's new. I think he needs people that are his."

"It would be interesting to hear what Sarah remembers," Delia agreed.

"So enough about me," Verna said. "How are you doing, Delia?"

Delia put her attention into wiping her hands on a towel, and her face pinked. "I have a date tonight."

"You what?" Verna shot her friend a grin. "Really? With who?"

"A man from Bird in Hand is coming to

take me driving this evening. And he will have dinner with my family." Delia laughed. "I was going to keep it a secret until I saw how it went, but... I have a hard time not opening up with you, Verna."

"I'm glad of that! You're cooking for him?" Verna asked. "That's...serious."

"He's wanting a wife," Delia replied. "And you're right—at our age, that's serious business. So I will cook for him, and my boys will be on their best behavior... I hope."

"Of course, they will be," Verna chuckled.

"Don't count on that." Delia shook her head. "They hate the idea of a new *daet*. They're upset with me for even agreeing to a date. I only told them about it this morning, and Moses is the only one who doesn't seem angry about it, but we'll see how he feels when he's faced with an actual man."

"Have you met him before?"

"Yah." Delia dropped her gaze. "With Adel. I went over there and sat down with him. He's a nice-looking man—tall, strong and with kind eyes. He was married for thirty years, and his wife passed. So he's looking for a new wife. He's lonesome."

"I think it sounds perfect," Verna said.

"I hope so... I do like him. But a brood of angry *kinner* is not going to endear me to him."

"He's a *daet*, isn't he?" Verna asked.

"*Yah*. He has three grown *kinner*—two daughters and a son."

"Then he should understand."

"But four sons—that's a different dynamic," Delia said, her earlier happiness fading. "They're very protective of me, and they've dug their heels in. Maybe I shouldn't have done this..."

"What did Adel say?"

"She thought it was worth trying. She said the boys need to get used to the idea."

"Then trust Adel," Verna said earnestly. "She's got good sense."

She had very good sense, and if she had reservations, she said so plainly, as Verna had discovered. She'd told Verna about Adam's reserved nature, hadn't she? She'd said that she worried he wouldn't soften very much... and those words still caused a tickle of anxiety in Verna's chest.

The children arrived then with the gray kitten snuggled in Amanda Rebecca's arms. One of Delia's middle sons, Aaron, came in behind them. He was a young teen with a splash of freckles across his face, and he leaned against the doorjamb that led into the mudroom.

"How is the stable, Aaron?" Delia asked.

"I finished everything," Aaron replied.

"The stalls are all clean, and I refilled the water buckets."

"*Danke*, son."

"*Yah.*" But Aaron's tone was dull. Verna cast him a veiled look. The boy was taller than his mother and broadening out, but there was still a lot of the boy left in his face. He pressed his lips together into a thin line and looked away.

Verna looked down at the kitten. She snuggled against Amanda Rebecca, who beamed up at Verna. At least Amanda Rebecca had been happy to have a new *mamm* in her life. Perhaps Verna should be more grateful for that. Delia was experiencing the opposite with her own *kinner*.

"I love my new kitten," Amanda Rebecca said earnestly. "I love her more than anything."

Verna smiled down at the girl. "I'm glad."

"She'll sleep in my bed, and I'll carry her everywhere!"

"Kittens like to run and play," Delia said. "Maybe you could play with her with a piece of yarn."

"*Yah?*" Amanda Rebecca smoothed a hand over her kitten's head. "I can do that! We have yarn—lots of it!"

"I imagine you do," Delia chuckled.

"How are the rest of the kittens, Moses?" Delia turned to her youngest son.

"Fine. They're playing all over the hay. It's hard to find them all now when I go in."

"They're growing up," Verna said, and she and Delia exchanged a knowing smile. It was wonderful to be able to do this with another mother. This was the world she'd longed to enter for years, and it was finally her turn to be a *mamm* amongst other *mamms*.

"I'll let you get back to cooking," Verna said, shooting Delia a smile. "I'll take this little one home, and we'll sort out a bed for the kitten in front of the stove."

"Oh, yes, to keep her warm!" Amanda Rebecca said. Then she turned to Delia. "Thank you for my kitten."

"You're very welcome, Amanda Rebecca," Delia said with a warm smile.

"Why are you making bread today, Mamm?" Aaron asked as Delia put on her boots.

"We need bread, son."

"Are you making it for *him*?" Aaron pressed.

Verna tried to pretend she couldn't hear.

"We'll discuss this in a few minutes." Delia sounded tired. "But I won't do anything that makes you boys miserable. You know that. Give him a chance."

Delia needed privacy for this conversation

with her boy, and Verna hurried Amanda Rebecca out the door.

"Goodbye!" Verna called over her shoulder. "We'll see you all again!"

Once Verna had Amanda Rebecca up in the buggy seat, the kitten cuddled close inside her coat, Verna flicked the reins and the horse started around, pulling the buggy back up the drive.

She looked over her shoulder once and saw Delia on the step, waving.

Delia had a date tonight…with a very nice man from another community. Verna had had a similar date before she married Adam, and she wondered if Delia would end up married shortly, too.

Delia was kind and full of energy. She was pretty, too, and a wonderful cook. She was also lonely since Zeke's death. It would be nice to see her with a man to take care of again. And whatever man managed to marry her would be blessed with a woman who knew how to have a happy marriage.

If only Verna could figure out the secret to a happy marriage with Adam. Was it just a matter of time? Or was there a secret to opening that man's heart? Verna truly wished she knew.

But in the meantime, she'd drop by her

parents' house. She sent up a silent prayer that her great-grandmother would be having a good memory day and she could give Delia a little insight into this family she'd married into.

That evening, Adam leaned back in the armchair next to a kerosene lamp in the sitting room. He could hear Verna in the kitchen, and the smells of roasted potatoes and a chicken casserole wafted out to where he sat.

"Her name is Smokey," Amanda Rebecca said, holding her kitten out.

Adam scooped up the little cat and looked down at her. She was a sweet kitten with big eyes and silken, dove-gray fur. "She does look rather smoky, doesn't she?"

"She's eaten some cat food from a can," Amanda Rebecca said. "And Mamm says we can give her hard cat food soon, too."

"Your *mamm* has it under control, I see," Adam said.

"Yah."

"Have you been learning your Bible verse?" he asked, handing the kitten back to her.

"What Bible verse?"

"The one you should be learning from Ephesians."

"No." Amanda Rebecca squinted at him.

He sighed. Of course. It had only been a week since the wedding, but he'd hoped that Verna would have been teaching her the verse all the same. It was important that Amanda Rebecca learn scripture. He wanted her to have it tucked away in her heart for when life got hard. He wanted her to have comfort at the ready.

Verna appeared in the doorway. "We have about half an hour until dinner. I'm sorry, Adam. I meant to have it on the table for when you got home, but I stopped by to see my parents on my way—"

"It's fine," he said. "It's okay. It smells wonderful."

"Danke." Her cheeks were pink from the heat of the stove. "My *mamm* and *daet* actually sent us home with the litter box for the kitten."

"That's very kind of them," he said.

Verna reached out and smoothed a hand over his daughter's hair. "Amanda Rebecca, why don't you go see if the kitten needs to use the litter box?"

"Yah, I should."

"It's how she'll learn," Verna said with a smile.

Amanda Rebecca headed off to the other room. He waited until Verna sat down on the edge of the couch opposite him.

"What is it?" he asked.

"My great-grandmother, as it turns out, knew your grandfather."

Adam leaned forward, resting his elbows on his knees. "Are you sure?"

"*Yah*. His name was Abram Lantz, correct? And your great-grandfather's name was Hezekiah Lantz. And his wife was Eve? And they lived on the Stoltzfus farm. She remembered them."

Adam's chest suddenly felt light and his breath caught in his throat. Those names all matched up. Was there really someone here in Redemption who remembered his family?

"She actually remembers them," he said, a smile tugging at his lips.

"*Yah*. Some days my great-grandmother doesn't seem to remember anything, but then she'll have days when she starts talking, and it's like it was yesterday for her. I realized that she might have known your family, and it turns out that she knew them personally. Her parents were friends with your great-grandparents."

Someone who'd known them! That was amazing unto itself, and he sent up a prayer of thanks for this serendipity.

"That's really something," he said. "What did she recall of them?"

"She remembered a lot, actually," Verna said, keeping her voice low. "They were good neighbors. There was a terrible drought one summer, and they had the biggest harvest out of anyone. So they shared it with their neighbors that winter. Everyone was deeply grateful to them."

Good neighbors... Yes, that was a good heritage.

"That's very nice to know," he murmured.

"But things didn't keep going so well for them after that," she said, and she licked her lips. "They died penniless."

He blinked. "What?"

"This is the part that...will be hard to hear." She rubbed at the knuckles on one hand nervously. "You don't have to hear it if you don't want to..."

She made this sound downright ominous. How bad could it be?

"I think I do have to hear it," he countered. "This is my family history in these parts, and you know how hard I've been looking for some scrap of information about my people. I want to know. What happened to them?"

"All right," Verna said softly. "There was some sort of family disagreement. My great-grandmother Sarah thought it was about who would inherit the farm. Their oldest son, or their youngest. The youngest wanted to farm. The oldest thought it should be his by right, even though he didn't want to farm."

"My grandfather Abram was the eldest," he said. "I know that much."

"*Yah*, that's what Sarah said," Verna confirmed. "And Abram was very upset that his father wouldn't leave him the farm. There was a lot of anger and bitterness between them."

"So Abram left home and came West?" Adam asked. It would be very sad indeed if he'd left his father's house in anger and never returned to make peace.

"Eventually he did go West, but not right away," Verna replied slowly. "Abram took some loans out with the farm as leverage against the debt, and—"

"Wait—how could he do that if he didn't own it?" Adam broke in. "It was his father's land, not his. His father must have taken the loan for him—"

"According to Sarah—" Verna swallowed and dropped her gaze "—he forged his father's signature as a cosigner. Sarah said that back then it was a lot easier to get away with these things. So he took out the loans, pocketed the money, and…that was when he left for Oregon."

Abram had stolen money…defrauded his own *daet*? Adam felt like he'd been kicked in the gut. When he sucked in a breath, there was a stab of pain under his ribs, and his mind twisted into a knot of disbelief. His grandfather was a thief? They were silent for a moment, the only sound that of Amanda Rebecca's voice from the other room, crooning to her kitten about how sweet she was.

"What about his parents?" Adam asked at last. "My great-grandparents?"

"No one knew where Abram had gone," she replied. "When the bank came calling, they had the choice to pay back the bank, or give their son up as a criminal who'd robbed them."

"And…?"

But he knew in his heart what they'd done. They did what any parent would do faced with their child's treachery. It was the same thing he'd do if his own daughter did something like that to him… What would he do for Amanda Rebecca? Absolutely anything!

"They paid back the bank," Verna said, and he nodded, knowing they would have. "It took selling the farm to the Stoltzfus family, who'd just moved to the area. Your great-grandparents Hezekiah and Eve rented a home after that with their other five *kinner*, and they were taken in by other relatives when they were too old to care for themselves. They had nothing left. They died early, Sarah said. Their hearts were broken."

"My grandfather Abram robbed his own parents..." he breathed. He rubbed his hands over his face. "That's...abominable."

She was silent, and he could almost feel her eyes on him. What must she think of the Lantzes as a family now?

"I had wanted to find family, but how can I do that now? I'm the grandson of a man who robbed his own *mamm* and *daet*. What about their other children—my great-aunts and great-uncles?"

"They moved away. Some went English." Verna paused for a moment. "Sarah says you have some distant cousins in the area..."

Adam didn't answer. What could he do with those family connections now? He wanted to show his daughter where their family came from on their Amish side, their faith stretching back into the distant past... their culture and way of life cementing them together as a family. He wanted to show her stability, integrity and a family history she could be proud of.

But the truth was nothing his daughter could be proud of... It was a sordid mess.

Verna slipped off the couch and came closer to where he sat, his elbows resting on his knees and his gaze locked on the floor. Her dress swung just within his vision.

"Adam, I'm sorry," she whispered.

"I should be the one apologizing to you," he said. "I didn't know any of this. And now you're a Lantz, too."

"You have no control over your ancestors," she replied. "The only man's behavior you can control is your own."

"Danke," he said. But it didn't help. The connection to the past, the link to a heritage—it was gone. Or perhaps it wasn't gone, at all. It was very firmly in place, but the heritage was one of shame.

"Mamm?" Amanda Rebecca called. "Something is burning!"

"Oh!" Verna looked at him, her eyes wide, and for a split second he had the impulse to grab her hand and keep her with him. Silly—dangerous, even! She turned and rushed from the room, and he sat there, listening to the sound of his wife and his daughter talking—Verna telling Amanda Rebecca to stand back, and the rattle of pan against stove top as she pulled it out of the oven.

This was the Amish home he'd longed for—happy, proper, appropriate. And now, he had very little to give back to his new wife. His name was supposed to be a source of pride for her, not something to avoid talking about. She'd wanted a husband of her own, a family of her own, and what kind of family had he given her?

Adam rested his head in his hands. He wished he could turn to her—tell her all that he was fearing, all that he was mourning right now. He wished he could put it all into words—even that seemed impossible. But he'd learned early in his last marriage that opening up with the mess inside of him was a recipe for disaster, and he wouldn't burden his new wife with his own tumbling emotions.

Gott, I have tried to do right. I have tried to choose wisely. I have tried to be an Amish man to the core, and every time I try, I fall short. In every way, I fall short...

He wasn't asking anything of Gott. What could he ask? His past was his past. His family history could not be undone. He wished it didn't hurt his pride so deeply as it did. Pride went before a fall. But what happened to a man with nothing left to be proud of?

Chapter Nine

Dinner that night was slightly burned, but still edible, and Verna watched as her husband ate his plateful silently, his eyes filled with sadness. She'd been the one to tell him the bad news, and she couldn't help but feel like his silent heartbreak was her fault, too.

After Amanda Rebecca and Smokey were tucked in for the night, Adam went around the house locking doors and turning out lights.

"Adam, it's okay," Verna said quietly. "It doesn't matter to me."

He flicked the lock on the side door. "I thought I had some Amish roots out here that would be better than the half-Amish roots I grew up with. My *mamm* tried hard. She did well. She loved us well…but she was always different. I was always the one who had the Englisher convert mother. And my grandfather on my *daet*'s side wouldn't talk about our heritage. He just didn't. And maybe it's cruel of me to be searching for more than my own parents gave me, but I wanted Amanda Rebecca to have a proper Amish life complete with deep, faithful Amish roots. And…that isn't your fault."

Verna undid her apron and took it off, hanging it up on a peg beside the kitchen cabinets. Adam had given his daughter a mother, but her ancestry would not include Verna. Not truly. She felt that sting, but she wouldn't let herself feel it. Not yet.

"Will we still look for your great-grandparents' graves this weekend?" she asked.

He paused at the bottom of the stairs, but he didn't answer right away.

"Because I think we should," she pressed on. "They are still your great-grandparents. They are still your family. I think we should find their graves."

"They're your family, too, now," he said.

"*Yah*, they are," she said. "But Adam, in this marriage, you also get my family. You get my parents, and grandparents, cousins, siblings, nieces and nephews… There are a lot of us, and I might have married into your family and taken your name, but you also get mine!"

Verna had connections, people who loved her and history here in Redemption. Her family went back seven generations in Pennsylvania, and before that, her family was in Switzerland. If he wanted roots, the Kauffmans had plenty!

"We both bring something to each other," she said earnestly. "And I have people here, Adam. That's what I bring. Connections and friendships and family."

"I know. And I truly appreciate that," Adam said. "I just have to get used to a new way of seeing my own history. That's all. I have to let go of a few boyish fantasies. I'll manage it. It just might take me until morning."

Verna put a hand on his arm, and he covered her hand with his warm palm. What she wanted was for him to come back into the kitchen and talk some more…or to ask her to go sit with him on the couch, or to simply eat some pie together, even if they were too full to want it. What she wanted was for him to turn toward her and *talk*.

His blue gaze met hers, and his lips parted as if he was about to say something, then they closed, and he gave her a polite nod.

"Good night," he said.

That was it? That was all he'd say to her?

"Good night," she said softly.

And as Verna watched her husband head up the stairs to his bedroom, a lump rose in her throat. It wasn't because of his family's sordid history, or because of any disappointment on her part related to his family. It was because he was walking away. In his sadness and frustration, he was closing her out.

It would always be this way, wouldn't it? He'd be a gentle, kind, considerate spouse. And no matter how much she longed for more depth, she wasn't going to get it. She should have listened to Adel's warning, but now it was too late. Verna had a new daughter she adored and a reserved husband with a tendency to keep to himself.

How was a woman supposed to love a man who turned away?

Saturday morning, Verna arranged for her mother to babysit Amanda Rebecca while Verna and Adam went to the Stoltzfus farm. At first Amanda Rebecca was silent and pale, but when Hannah pulled out a new Amish doll and a little basket of thumbprint cookies, a smile wreathed the girl's face, and she excitedly told her new *mammi* all about her kitten, Smokey. They would be just fine.

But as they pulled away from the house in

the buggy, Verna felt her heart tug back toward the little girl, and she realized in a rush that in this short time she'd truly become a mother.

"She'll be fine," Adam said, as if reading her mind.

"I know." Verna turned forward again. "I'm glad I have my family here. This makes everything easier for me, you know."

"*Yah*, I know."

"I never really understood how a family supported a marriage before this," she admitted. "But it helps a woman to know that she has people around her to assist with her duties and not judge her for not being enough."

"Verna, I don't think anyone could judge you. You're everything I prayed for in a mother for my daughter."

"*Danke.*" But what about a wife for himself? Was she everything he'd prayed for there, too? She didn't dare ask. Instead she said, "I'm glad you asked me to come with you today."

"We're a family now, you and me," he said, and he smiled.

They were… Perhaps she needed to slow down her hopes for their relationship. Delia was right—she had the rest of her life ahead of her to build up her marriage.

"Do you have any hints about where the graves might be found?" she asked.

"Moe said that there's a dilapidated little house in the woods. He never found graves, but it's a start."

She nodded. "It does sound that way."

When they arrived at the farm, Moe and Adam chatted a little bit while Adam unhitched the horse and got him some hay and water.

"Verna, will you be visiting with Ellen?" Moe asked, turning a kindly smile onto her.

"No, Moe," Verna said. "I'll be going with my husband."

"Ah." Moe's smile spread across his face. "Now that has a nice ring to it, doesn't it? Good. I hope the two of you have a nice time together. And that you find what you're looking for."

What they were looking for... Adam was looking for some connection to his ancestors in spite of his grandfather's sins, but Verna was looking for some sort of connection to her husband. May Gott bless both of their efforts today.

"To find that old house, it's past a huge fir tree," Moe said. "The house is hidden behind it—about fifty yards into the woods. The tree is very large. It's hard to miss this time of year when the other trees around it are bare."

"Danke," Adam said. "That's a help."

The morning was overcast and gray, but the wind wasn't overly cold, and Verna's knitted scarf kept her plenty warm. She noticed the red in Adam's cheeks from the wind, and she realized that he could use a warm scarf, too. She'd been knitting for Amanda Rebecca, but she'd have to knit him one, as well. As they tramped through the snow, Verna walked a little faster to keep up with Adam's longer strides.

Verna looked around at the farmyard. There were some outbuildings, a stable, a barn farther on, a coop. Some of the buildings needed work—the house certainly could use another coat of paint and the chicken coop looked like it needed to be replaced completely. But none of these buildings had been standing for a hundred years or more. There was no sign of the old farm from generations ago.

"They used to build beside the old place," Verna added. "Your folks would stay in the old house, and you'd build a newer house a little ways off—a bit of privacy for the new marriage, too. I think that old cabin in the woods is likely your great-grandparents' house from when they started out here."

Adam stopped and turned around. "I think you're right. The trees might have grown up around the old place. So if we start looking along the tree line for that massive fir…"

There was a small pasture beyond the barn with three cows lingering close by a feeder. And beyond the pasture, forest. A few snowflakes spun down from the sky, and Verna started to breathe hard as they entered the field, their boots sinking into deeper snow.

"Here—" Adam held his hand out, and she caught his gloved hand with her own.

He was stronger than she was, and walking with his added support did make it easier. This was the first time she'd held his hand, and she suddenly felt bashful. He held her hand like he had a right to it—and he certainly did—but she'd never been touched quite like that before.

"Are you okay?" Adam slowed, his grip the same firm grasp.

"Yah." She tried to fight the blush in her cheeks, but her face only got warmer.

"Are you sure?" He released her hand then, and she wished that he wouldn't.

"It's just that we've never—"

He looked down at his gloved hand and a smile quirked at one side of his lips. "Held hands?"

She felt foolish now for saying anything. He was her husband, and holding her hand was certainly the least of his rights.

"I've wanted to," he said quietly. "But I didn't want to push things too fast."

"We've been married more than a week," she said. "I don't think holding hands is rushing it."

He chuckled at her dry humor. "Okay, then. I'll start holding your hand, if you're okay with it."

"Yah." She couldn't help but smile. "That would be nice."

The wind picked up again, and she tugged her scarf a little closer around her neck.

"Let's get to the trees," he said, holding his hand out to her again. "That'll shelter us from the worst of it."

She reached back, and he caught her gloved hand. It felt nice—his strength tugging her along as they picked up their pace again. Adam held her hand firmly, pulled her closer against him as they walked. She liked it. She felt like she belonged to him this way—his powerful stride carrying her along with him. Suddenly, the wind wasn't quite so cold.

"You know, I meant what I said before about my family being yours, too," Verna said, puffing along beside him. "My parents are so happy to have Amanda Rebecca as their new granddaughter, and I know my family was a bit of a blur at Service Sunday, but you'll get to know them all better."

"I know," he said, casting her a faint smile.

"Whatever happened on this farm all those years ago doesn't matter," she added.

"Oh, it matters." His voice was low, curt. "It matters a lot. But I should face it, at least."

"Your grandfather's mistakes aren't yours!" she pressed.

"But it explains a lot," he countered. "I grew up without family stories. Do you know what that's like—to have no stories of your grandfather from his childhood, no stories of your great-grandparents, as if they'd never lived? I heard stories from my Englisher side! My *mamm* told me about her father, who owned a gas station, and her grandfather who was a miner, and her great-grandfather who was an alcoholic... Families come with stories. That's how they work. To only find out about where your family lived because you look it up at a historical society..." He blew out a breath that hung frozen in the air. "Before my grandfather died, I begged him to tell me stories about himself, and he refused. I thought it was me... I thought I was a disappointment to him. But it turns out, it was him. He was the disappointment."

She could feel the anger emanating out of him. "I'm sorry. That sounds awful for a boy to think his granddad didn't like him."

"It affected my *daet*, too. He left the faith for a while and went English. He married my *mamm* and ended up bringing her back with him before we were born, but our family was always the odd one." Adam was breathing hard now, too, as they approached the tree line. The wind was less by the trees, and Adam stopped at the underbrush.

"But she did return with him," Verna pointed out. "That's amazing—an Englisher woman to embrace our way of life."

"Embrace it? *Yah*, but always with an accent, so to speak," he said. "She was always different. She didn't speak Pennsylvania Dutch very well. She didn't understand our way of doing things. She tried, and she was supportive of Daet, but her cooking was different, and her way of seeing the world would never be like the rest of the community. My grandfather was very critical of her. I love my mother deeply, but my grandfather's reticence affected his relationship with everyone—my *daet*, my *mamm*, my grandmother…"

"What happened to all that money?" she asked.

Adam shrugged. "I've asked myself that, too, because when my grandfather died when I was a young teen, there was nothing left. All I can think is that he stole it and Gott didn't bless it. It was frittered away—the ill-gotten gains that had cost my grandfather everything, possibly even his own soul."

Verna looked back across the pasture. The house blurred through the steadily falling snow. She felt Adam's thumb move over the top of her hand, and when she looked back at him, his eyes were filled with regret.

"It was the past," she said softly. "Before you were even born!"

"His sins, yes. But I was critical of my *mamm*, too," Adam admitted. "I know that my grandfather's sins are his own. But it's what I did that eats at me. I thought my grandfather must be right, that Mamm wasn't Amish enough, and that she needed to do better."

"Oh, Adam…" She sighed.

"I was critical of her when she got things wrong in the language, or when she didn't understand a joke, or when she cooked food that was too Englisher, like spaghetti or pizza." He licked his lips. "I was angry because her being different made me different, too, and I didn't want to be different. My first language was English, because it's what my mother spoke to me. I was Amish, and I wanted the security of a rooted Amish life. I still want that. I've come looking for some sort of Amish ancestry that I could own and relate to out here in Redemption. But what has my criticism done to my *mamm*?"

Adam dropped her hand, and Verna looked up at him, breathless. This was what she'd wanted—to see what was stewing around inside of him, and then as he looked down at her, she saw those windows shut again.

"Adam, I've had attitudes I wasn't proud of, either," she said quickly. She'd spoken before she'd even thought it through, but she didn't want this brief intimacy to end.

"Yah?"

"For me, I had some very hard feelings against the Englishers. I thought they were worldly and quite wicked. They scared me."

"And now you teach their *kinner* to knit."

She couldn't read his tone—but she plunged on. "I hated it at first. I thought that I was simply doing a good deed for some heathen, but I realized they aren't so different from us."

"They are very different," he countered.

"Their beliefs are different," she agreed.

"Their goals, too. But at a heart level, these at-risk youth are just big *kinner* who want to be accepted and loved. That's it. Like your *mamm*. She's been raised Englisher. That won't go away. But at heart—she's your mother who loves you."

"*Yah*, you are right about that."

"Your grandfather didn't see the most important part of her," she said quietly. "Her heart."

"I wish I'd stood up for her when I was young," he said. "I wish I'd defended her. To have faced his judgment all while raising her little ones in a culture that would never fully understand her... I can't imagine how hard that was. And yet she did it, and she's still Amish, standing by my *daet* and working the farm they bought together."

"But you were young. You weren't a man yet," she said, and she paused for a moment. "I learned to be easier on the Englishers, and as I learned to be easier on them, I also learned to be easier on myself."

And that had perhaps been the biggest relief of all.

"You deserve that," he said gently, and the wind whipped up again, snow swirling around them.

It was easy to forget how young he'd been when his brother had died. It was funny how a man could look back on his childhood self and expect adult responses from him. Would he expect it from other *kinner*? From Amanda Rebecca? Never. But Adam still felt that strange sense of responsibility. He was glad she'd learned to be gentler on herself, but he wasn't sure he could allow himself the same. He was a man, and it was his job to protect his family. That didn't come by being easy on himself.

He shielded his eyes as he looked deeper into the woods. The bare deciduous trees grew straight and tall, except for a few that leaned into each other, the last stage of a tree's life before it slid to the forest floor and became the home of small animals and fungi. Snow capped the twigs and boughs, and the spattering of evergreen trees stood out like giants guarding the rest. Was there one larger than the others?

"Let's keep going this way," he said, turning his back to the wind. The direction was just as good as any other, except they wouldn't have snow blown into their faces. Verna fell into step beside him. He reached out and caught her hand again. This wasn't for her this time—not to help her catch up through the deep snow. This was for him, because holding her hand was a strange comfort, and there was no one out here to watch them. Their breath hung in the air in front of them and then whipped away in the swirling wind.

He stole a look at her, and her cheeks had grown even pinker than they'd been in the cold. She held his hand just as tightly as he held hers. Walking along the tree line just gave him the excuse, and for a few minutes, he wasn't really paying much attention to the trees beyond, just to the pressure of her fingers in his hand, and to the feeling of her arm brushing up against his coat sleeve.

But then he spotted it. Just as they crested a low hill—the farm buildings behind them, disappearing into the swirling whiteness—ahead, down the slope, he saw a large green tree rising up from behind the bare deciduous trees in front of it. It was broad and full, and its top rose far above the rest of the forest canopy. He stopped short.

"Oh!" Verna breathed.

"I think that's it," he said.

"It must be…"

They started down the hill, and the wind picked up at the same time, changing direction and coming full into their faces with a slap of snow, and then rushing at their backs again. A storm was picking up, and Adam could only hope that it wouldn't last long. All the same he pressed forward, tugging Verna closer against him as they came down the hill. There was an opening in the brown, scraggly undergrowth, and he led the way into the trees. The wind was somewhat less in the woods, and he angled his steps in the direction of that massive fir tree. He stepped over, some logs, but there did seem to be a path through here, albeit a little overgrown. He stopped to help Verna over a fallen tree, and as she cleared it, her breath coming fast, he spotted a moss-covered shape a couple of yards behind that behemoth of a fir tree.

It was indeed a small house. Half of it was crumpled and rotted away, but a front door, a small window with no glass and thick log walls remained. It was a single story with a sloping roof and a stone chimney coming out the top as straight and commanding as if the house around it was still new. This was it—his great-grandparents' house. Had all five of their children slept under that roof at the same time? It hardly looked large enough, but then the older generations shared beds and simply made do.

Wind whistled overhead, but nestled behind the tree in the woods it was warmer and less blustery. He released Verna's hand and walked up to the front of the house. The door was ajar, the hinges rusted to the color of pennies. He gave the door frame a shake, and it was still solid. Then he stepped inside the house.

Adam's eyes took a moment to adjust to the dimness, but once they did, he was met with a strangely domestic scene. Moss crawled up one wall and along a windowsill. Dried leaves moldered in the corners, and a spider web hung down from a crossbeam; he batted it down. A solid wooden table stood to one side with a chair turned upside down on top of it. There was a potbellied stove with a broken stove pipe next to the table, and a big, stone fireplace dominated the far wall. Cupboard doors hung on broken hinges, and inside one of them he could see some dust-covered bottles with unnameable dark liquids inside, long since gone rancid.

"We found it," Verna said behind him.

He turned and saw her gaze moving over the walls and stopping at the far side of the room where the roof ended, and a space of daylight filtered through. The rest of the house—bedrooms and whatever else had been over there—had collapsed, and two trees now grew up through the broken roof, pushing up into the air beyond.

"We did… My great-grandfather would have built this house with his own two hands."

He could almost feel that family connection in the timbers of the walls, in the crossbeams in the ceiling, in each stone of the fireplace. He could feel it in the planning, the layout, the hopes and dreams that would have gone into this small house that had supported a man and his wife as they faced the elements in Pennsylvania farmland. And here he was with his own new wife, standing on the very floorboards—sagging, but still there—his great-grandfather had laid.

"And it stood up rather well," she murmured. "This was a well-made house."

"Yah…" Well-made, but a house with heartbreak, too. This was the house they lost, the home their son had swindled away from them.

Adam went over to the table and pulled the chair off the top of it. It was still solid enough, and he found an old milk crate underneath the table. That was newer—probably brought by Moe's sons when they discovered the old place.

"I didn't mean to burden you earlier," Adam said. "I shouldn't have said all of that."

"What do you mean, burden me?" she asked.

"I mean—" He closed his mouth. He shouldn't be talking as much as he was about family problems. "I mean, our marriage is new. I don't need to unload every heartbreak when I talk to you. We have time for that."

"It's not a burden," she said. "It helps me understand you."

"There's more to me than past pain," he countered.

She nodded. "*Yah.* I know."

The truth was, he wanted to start fresh with Verna—let the past stay in the past and have something sweet and new with her. Verna crossed the room, ducking under a low beam, and stopped at his side.

"I want us to have a happy home," she said softly. "I want my family to be your family, and for you to find your place here. And I want us to buy a farm, if that's what you want. I want to raise *kinner*, and to know each other better than anyone else in all this world."

"Me, too," he said.

She was so close, so soft, and she smelled of homemade soap and sweetness. She wanted a beautiful, peaceful life, and he longed to provide it for her. He reached out and took her hand, pulling her glove off her fingers. Then he lifted her fingers to his lips and pressed a kiss against them.

It had been impulsive, and it was the first time he'd kissed her, but standing out here in this tiny log house filled with history and someone else's memories, it felt right. Verna's lips parted, and she seemed to be holding her breath.

"I'd wanted to give you a family legacy to be proud of under your married name," he said, his voice low. "It looks like it won't be so easy to provide, though. So, I'll do my best to start fresh with you—build on to a newer legacy. I still want Amanda Rebecca to look at our home and see the kind of happiness she wants for herself one day."

"I want that, too," she said.

"And I want…" He licked his lips, looking down at her upturned face. "I want to kiss you."

"Oh…" Her breath seemed to whoosh out of her, and she looked up at him, frozen.

"Is that okay?" he whispered.

She nodded mutely and stared up at him wide-eyed. It wasn't like he could kiss her when she was staring at him like that, but now that he'd warned her, he couldn't very well not kiss her, either. Besides, he'd been wondering how he could cross that divide with her—and he did want to kiss her.

"Maybe you could…close your eyes," he said with a soft laugh.

A smile touched her lips, but she did as he asked and shut her eyes, her lashes brushing her cheeks. He pulled off his gloves and tossed them on the table, then ran his fingers over her wind-chilled face. Her chest rose and fell with her breath, and he felt a tenderness toward her that almost scared him. He lowered his lips over hers. For a moment, she didn't move at all, and then she leaned toward him ever so slightly in encouragement. Her lips were soft, and she didn't kiss him back, but she didn't pull away, either. When he pulled back, her eyes blinked open and she looked up at him, breathless.

"Was that okay?" he asked.

She nodded. "*Yah.* That was very nice."

"You could…return the kiss," he suggested, and felt almost too forward saying it out loud. But they were married, after all, and they should be able to speak of such things as kissing.

"Okay." Her cheeks flamed red, and she rose up onto her tiptoes and placed a chaste kiss on his lips. His heart nearly flipped over in his chest from the sweetness of the gesture.

That wasn't quite what he'd meant…but perhaps he'd have to show her.

"Can we try again?" he asked.

She nodded, and this time when he leaned over her, her eyes fluttered shut. He gathered her up in his arms and kissed her again. It was just a whisper more familiar, and this time when he kissed her, she did kiss him back, just a little, and his chest filled with butterflies. Her lips were warm and soft, and her breath was featherlight against his face. When he pulled back this time, a smile touched her lips.

He'd been dreaming of this, hoping for it, unsure how to achieve it, and he felt like he'd finally stepped across a gulf that separated them. It was a start in this marriage.

"Maybe we can do that more often," he said.

She nodded. "Okay."

And he felt his own face heating. "You are quite beautiful, Verna."

He meant it with every fiber of his being. He wished he could say more—tell her that she was beautiful and intimidating, and so gentle and kind that he felt he almost didn't deserve her. But he stopped at beautiful.

"No one has ever said that before," she said.

No one? Were they all blind?

"Then I shall say it," he said. "And you are."

The snow outside had stopped falling, and in the place of the whistling of wind, he could hear the twitter of birds in the trees overhead. It was time to go back to warmth and community again, but he found himself smiling all the same.

He'd just kissed his wife, and he felt as elated as a young buck.

Chapter Ten

That evening, Verna stood at the kitchen sink washing dishes. Adam was outside finishing up in the stable, and upstairs Amanda Rebecca was supposed to be trying to sleep, but Verna could hear the girl singing to herself.

Verna washed the last dish, dried it and let the water out of the sink. Then she hung up her towel and headed up the stairs. Amanda Rebecca's singing stopped, and Verna poked her head into the girl's bedroom.

"It's okay to sing, honey," Verna said.

"It is?"

"As long as you're singing sleepy songs," Verna said.

Amanda Rebecca smiled up at her. "Okay."

Verna shut the door and Amanda Rebecca's little piping voice started up again—a church hymn with the wrong words, but her tiny heart was in the right place.

She went down the hall to her own bedroom and went inside. She opened her hope chest and looked down at the remaining items. She'd already brought out linens and towels, dishes and a proper copper tea kettle. Now stacked neatly in the bottom of the cedar-lined chest were little baby items—booties, sleepers, bibs, glass bottles... All in preparation for a different time in a married woman's life.

She shut the lid gently. One day, she did hope to have a baby of her own. But Gott had already blessed her with so much that she wouldn't tarnish it with hoping for more just now. She'd cherish her husband's kisses and those soft songs sung by her stepdaughter. There was much to be thankful for.

Verna settled into her chair with her knitting. She was making a new scarf—a black one for Adam. She wanted him to be warm, and to think of her when he bundled up. Her needles clacked cheerily as she knit, and her heart soared upward toward Gott.

She was truly thankful for this family Gott had blessed her with. Truly and deeply.

A few minutes later she heard Adam come back inside and his footsteps on the stairs. She paused, listening as the creaks of the floorboards stopped in the hallway.

"Adam?" she said softly.

He pushed open her door. His hair was rumpled from his hat, and he smoothed a hand down his beard—the one place that didn't need smoothing—and she couldn't help but smile.

"I'm knitting this for you," she said.

"Yah?"

She nodded. "I think you could use a warm scarf."

"I wanted to…" He cleared his throat. "I mean… I…" He cleared his throat again, and she stopped her knitting, looking at him. His cheeks pinked. "I hoped to kiss you goodnight."

"Oh." She put down her knitting, suddenly feeling flustered. "Okay."

Adam came over to where she sat, bent down, touched her chin with his finger to tip her face upward and kissed her lips gently. He met her gaze then, direct, warm.

"Are you…tired?" he asked.

"Not yet. I've got a lot to knit."

"Ah."

"Are you?" she asked.

"Somewhat." He straightened.

"You do work hard, Adam," she said.

He paused again, his blue gaze meeting hers, and for a moment, they just looked at each other. It was like he was waiting for something.

"Are you happy with how things are?" he asked.

"*Yah*, very."

"With…your room?" he asked.

She wouldn't dream of criticizing this bedroom in any way. She knew how hard Adam and Amanda Rebecca had worked putting it together for her.

"It's perfect, Adam. I love it."

He pressed his lips together and nodded a couple of times.

"Good night," she said, unsure what else to say, and it felt like something needed to be said.

Adam paused for a beat, not moving, then he nodded again. "*Yah*. Good night, Verna."

Adam left her room and closed her door with a gentle click behind him, and Verna sat there with her knitting on her lap and her lips moist from his. Why did she feel like that kiss was asking for more? More of her. More of her heart.

But if it were, he wouldn't have left, would he?

From the other room Amanda Rebecca's singing paused, there was the sound of a yawn, and then quiet. She picked up her knit-

ting needles again. She'd finish this scarf tonight—she was a fast knitter, after all. And
tomorrow, he'd have a tangible reminder that
his wife cared.

The weekend passed quickly, and Monday
evening, Verna was dropped off at the community center by Adam and Amanda Rebecca, who were going to do some grocery
shopping at the big supermarket in town while
she taught her class.

Adam wore his scarf, which sent a warm
wave through Verna's heart. It was her own
work, worn by her husband. This was what
she'd wanted, wasn't it?

When Verna arrived, a social worker was
waiting for her. Graham Stout was one of the
community workers who oversaw her class,
and he smiled when she came into the room.

"Miss Kauffman," he said.

"Just Verna," she said for maybe the tenth
time. But Englishers didn't understand.

"Verna. Of course." He shook her hand—
something she still wasn't used to, but these
particular Englishers felt it was rude not to
shake her hand. "Cherie Reynolds is going
before a judge, and we need some paperwork
filled out so that she can prove she's done her

court-ordered class work." He passed her an envelope.

"Blade is done?" Verna's heart skipped a beat. "What now?"

"Well, after we prove it to the judge, she needs to stay out of trouble and hopefully this will be the end of it."

The end of it… Somehow that was hard to imagine with these teens. They needed love and support, but turning that corner and living a whole new life would be very difficult for them.

"She has a job now at a burger place," Verna said.

"Yes, I know," Graham said. "And she's attended all her therapy sessions, too. She's doing well. I'm hopeful."

Hopeful was as good as it got in this field of work, Verna had learned. But hope was no small thing, either. Verna opened the envelope and scanned down the form that needed filling. At the bottom, there was a box for her to fill out any thoughts she had about her student.

"I might need more space than that," Verna said. "I have so many good things to say about Blade…or Cherie, I should say. I hope they let her see it."

"The focus is on rehabilitation," Graham

said. "I'm sure they will show her. And thank you for your contributions here, Verna. These kids talk about your knitting class like it's something sacred."

And maybe it was sacred—these tender, vulnerable hearts coming here to learn a skill that didn't come easily to them. They were here to learn how to apply themselves, how to talk respectfully and how to be part of a community.

"I wonder what she'll do with herself." Verna said.

"The toughest part is finding a community," Graham said. "Their old friends were often their problem—people who encouraged them in bad habits and bad choices. So breaking those contacts and finding new, more positive friends is both really important and really hard. A lot of the time, going on the right path means going it alone."

"We don't believe in that," Verna said. "I mean, we do believe in doing the right thing, even if you do it alone, but we also believe in community. We need people around us to build us up. We were created for it."

"Created for it or not," Graham said. "Not everyone gets that."

"Not you?" she asked, looking at the young man quizzically.

"Well…not really. My wife and I moved here from out of state. We know a few people, I guess. I wouldn't call it a community. You Amish have something really beautiful. Never take that for granted. Because doing it our way is a whole lot harder."

"I hope Blade finds her community," Verna said earnestly.

She prayed for it, and she also prayed that Gott would protect Verna's own community, too. Because Verna didn't know how she'd face all these changes and challenges without them!

Graham took his leave, and Verna set up the chairs in a circle. Then she sat down with her form and began to fill it out very carefully in black pen. She double-checked dates from her own record book, and then she wrote as small as she could in the box asking for her comments.

Cherie Reynolds is an intelligent, kind, sweet young woman. She works hard on her knitting, and she's eager to help others learn, too. She's considerate and thoughtful, and it has been my true honor to teach her this valuable skill.

And yet, that didn't even encompass what she wanted to say about Blade…to Blade.

She has developed friendships here, and

I, for one, shall deeply miss her. I wish her nothing but happiness and blessings in her future.

She'd known that she'd need to say good-bye to these young people when she started teaching the class, and somehow a lump rose in her throat at the thought.

The door opened, and she looked up to see the first of her students arriving—Harry and Tia. They headed over to the circle, chatting together, then cast Verna a smile.

"What's wrong, Miss Verna?" Tia asked. "You look sad."

"Oh, I'm fine," Verna said, tucking her paperwork back into the envelope. She'd have to deliver this to the social services office the next day.

Abigail and Jolene entered next. They came over to their habitual seats in the circle, and the young people settled in together and pulled out their knitting.

"Does anyone need more yarn?" Verna asked.

"I'm getting low in mine," Jolene said. "I think I'm almost done with this scarf."

"I'll show you how to cast off, and you can start a new one," Verna said. "You've done so well, Jolene! You're a natural."

"I'm definitely not a natural," Tia said.

"That's not true," Jolene said. "I think you're doing really well. I like your scarf."

Tia looked down at her work skeptically. It had little holes all through it from dropped stitches.

"In fact, when you're finished it, I'll wear it," Jolene added. "I'll give you mine. You give me yours. I'll wear it with pride, girl."

Tears welled up in Tia's eyes, and Verna stood back, watching the interaction. These young people had come a long way since their first hesitant meeting together when they'd been introduced to knitting needles, yarn and their Amish teacher.

Blade arrived last. She pulled her backpack off her shoulder and dropped it next to her chair.

"Hey," she said. "Sorry, I'm late."

"You're not late," Verna said. "You're right on time."

"At my job, they say anything after five minutes early is late," Blade said, but she shot Verna a brilliant smile.

"You got a job?" Harry asked. "Where?"

The conversation turned to Blade's new job, and how she hated uniforms, but her new boss hadn't made her take out her piercings or cover her tattoos, so she was grateful.

"You know, I was working at an ice cream

place that made me cover up my tattoos, even in the hot summer weather," Abigail said. "I think that's cruelty."

"I wouldn't cover mine," Harry said. "They're meaningful. They're a part of me."

"They're 'unprofessional,'" Blade said, making air quotes with her fingers.

"Would you cover your tattoos if you had some?" Tia asked, turning to Verna, and Verna just blinked at them.

"I—" She shook her head. "I don't even know what to say."

"Oh, leave her alone," Abigail said with a laugh. "Poor Miss Verna. She can't even imagine having a tattoo!"

"I can't," Verna confessed. "But… I do understand you needing to stand by who you are, and what's important to you. As an Amish woman, I stand out all the time when I go into the city. People stare at me. It might not be a tattoo, but my clothing shows that I'm different, and I won't change it to blend in."

The young people grew silent, and they looked over at her thoughtfully.

"It just comes down to what you stand for," Verna said, and then she pulled out her own knitting needles and the little mittens she'd started for Amanda Rebecca. "Let's get knitting." She looked around the circle of young Englishers, and her heart swelled with love. "I've missed all of you. Tattoos and all."

They laughed then, and so did Verna. This was the last class they'd all be together in this particular group, and she knew that tonight was special.

When they all graduated from her class and moved on with their lives, she'd miss them. But she'd also be happy for them. And she sent up a silent prayer that Gott would bless these tender, vulnerable souls and show them His love.

Adam walked around the supermarket with his daughter at his side. They picked up the items they needed—crackers, lettuce, fresh vegetables, peanut butter, marshmallows, canned tuna and a package of chicken legs... He worked off the list Verna had left for him.

He noticed an Englisher woman aiming her camera at him, and he nudged his daughter in front of him, out of sight. The Englishers were only curious—he understood that—but having his daughter filmed was not only against their faith, it was unsettling. His mother used to say that they didn't understand, but all the same, he remembered how her hand used to tighten on his when Englishers would stare and snap pictures with disposable cameras—the popular option twenty-five years ago. And his mother would know—she used to be an Englisher. She used to be a curious outsider looking in at them before she married his *daet*.

Days like this one, Adam missed his mother desperately. He missed her smiles, her cooking, her advice... He missed her jokes that were never quite Amish enough, and the fact that he could trust her with anything. He wanted her to meet Verna. He wanted her advice, because his mother always said that women were women, regardless of what culture they were born into.

Some things are universal, son.

But were they, really? Had she been right about that? They'd never had a pack of Amish *kinner* chase a boy into a frozen runoff before...

Adam caught Amanda Rebecca's hand. He felt better holding her warm fingers in his palm. He'd only been a boy when his brother died, but he was a man now, and his protective instinct when it came to his daughter was fierce.

He took his time with shopping, not wanting to arrive at the community center too early, but by the time they'd gone through the checkout and he'd loaded the groceries into the back of the buggy, there was still plenty of time to spare.

"I think we're going to arrive there early," Adam said.

"We can go inside and visit!" Amanda Rebecca said. "It's fun. You'll like it."

"I don't know... I don't want to interrupt her class," he said, more to himself than to his daughter. He also didn't want to expose Amanda Rebecca to more of the Englisher influence, but he had to admit that he was curious.

The streets were wet with melting snow, and there weren't too many cars on the road, for which he was grateful. When he got to the community center, he parked in a buggy parking spot and tied up the horse. He stood for a moment, wondering if he should look inside, when his daughter said, "Daet, I can show you her room." Amanda Rebecca leaned out the door, big blue eyes fixed on him. "I know where it is, you know."

Yah, she would. He paused, then gave up his pretense. He did want to see what Verna's class looked like. And maybe he owed his *mamm* this much, too.

"Okay," he conceded. "We'll just peek."

Amanda Rebecca led the way into the

building. They passed a sign for an AA meeting going on, and the murmur of voices filtered out into the stuffy hallway. His daughter carried on past that room and down a long hallway. One door stood open, and he could see a handwritten sign taped to it that read Amish Knitting—Monday and Wednesday, 7:00 p.m.

That would be hers, and he reached out and caught Amanda Rebecca's hand again.

"Let's not interrupt," he said softly.

"Okay," she whispered back.

Adam quietly approached the room, and he peeked in the door. No one seemed to see him—all the heads were bowed over knitting, and he recognized the girl from the burger joint working with her needles. She looked frustrated, and Verna scooted her chair over, took the needles from her hands and helped to sort it out. The other Englisher teens looked similar—dressed in jeans with boots, leather, dyed hair, ratty backpacks… A whole lot like that pack of kids who'd picked on Jonah. His stomach knotted at the memory.

"Tonight is the last night Blade will be with us," Verna said, setting aside her knitting. "And I just want to say how much I have enjoyed her presence in my class these last eight weeks. Blade, I'm very proud of all you have accomplished."

"This is it?" a girl asked. "Really? I'm gonna miss you!"

"Hey, my court-assigned duty is complete," Blade said, but she cast Verna a wobbly smile. "I'll miss you, too."

"I didn't understand why the courts would want to send you *kinner* to an Amish teacher," Verna said. "But you all have changed me as much as this class has helped you. You've made me a better woman."

"I don't believe that for a second!" one girl said. "You were already perfect, Miss Verna."

"Perfect?" Her voice stayed soft. "Not even close. But I'm so glad we all got this time together. The group will change. We'll get more students, and the rest of you will finish your time here. But since the court sent you to an Amish Christian woman, I'm going to err on the side of my conscience and say this…"

Everyone stilled, and Adam held his breath.

"I pray that Gott goes with you every step of your life," Verna said. "I pray that He shows you how precious you are. I pray He helps you to make the brave choice and stand tall, each one of you. And if you are ever in trouble, I hope you drop to your knees and ask Him to help you. And after that…"

Verna leaned forward, her gaze moving over the group of teens. "I'm going to be practical now, because I know that matters to you all. If you are ever in trouble—if you don't have a place to go, and you don't have food to eat… if you're tempted to steal, or to go along with something you know is wrong, I want you to go to the nearest church."

"Church?" It was a boy who said that. He sounded surprised.

"Church." Her voice remained firm. "You ask to talk to a minister, and you tell him your problem. He'll find you food, or get you shelter. He'll help you stay strong and keep to the right path. I'm not the only Christian who will love you. I promise you that. There's a whole world full of us!"

This was not quite Amish theology. The Amish way was the right way. There was no other option. And yet his *mamm* had been a Christian woman out there with the Englishers, hadn't she? For a moment, Adam's practical mind warred with his heart, but he understood what she was doing. What were city-living youngsters supposed to do in a time of crisis—go to the nearest Amish farm? She was giving them the advice she might give to some rebellious teens in their *Rumspringa*. She was giving them a practical solution to problems she knew would arise. And she was sharing the responsibility of these Englisher teens with the Englisher Christians.

"I think I'd freak them out!" Blade chuckled. "Look at me! They'd faint!"

Adam nearly had… He'd only seen the outside, and she'd been intimidating, all right.

"They're made of sterner stuff than you think," Verna said. "You might have shocked me a little bit, my sweet Blade, but I'm more easily shocked than most. And look how much I adore you now!"

"With tattoos and piercings?" another girl said. "You sure?"

"Tia, I'm positive. We all need help sometimes. Every last one of us, and if you are in trouble, I want you to remember me— an Amish lady who truly loved each one of you—and follow my advice. Go to a church. You will find kindness there, and hope, and a solution. I promise you that."

Suddenly Adam saw what Verna saw. Beyond the clothing, the hair, the makeup…beyond the piercings and Englisher ways, these were *kinner*. They were young and foolish, and when they looked at Verna, those insolent stares softened. They loved her… They looked to her for answers, and as an Amish woman so very different from them, she could say things that no one else could say to them.

She could point them to Gott.

"And I do hope you keep knitting, Blade," Verna said.

"I can't promise that, Miss Verna," the girl said with a half smile. "The knitting hasn't gotten any easier, and I don't think I'll ever finish this scarf. But I can promise that if I really get into deep trouble, I'll find a church. For you."

Verna put a hand over her heart. "*Danke.* It means the world to me." And then Verna lifted her gaze, and her face suddenly lit up as she spotted Adam and Amanda Rebecca. "Oh, my husband and daughter are here!"

Everyone turned.

"Everyone, this is my husband, Adam," Verna said. "And you all know Amanda Rebecca already."

"Hey, girl," Blade said, shooting Amanda Rebecca a grin.

Adam's daughter slipped out of his grasp and headed over to the group of teenagers. She beamed up at them and leaned against Blade's knee. She was comfortable there—far too comfortable—and his stomach knotted.

"Come in, Adam," Verna said, and Adam suddenly felt out of place—boots and work pants, and his Amish felt hat.

"Nice to meet you," a teen girl said. "We've heard really nice things about you."

"Just be good to Verna," the teenage boy said, leaning back and giving him a challenging stare. The boy meant what he said. "She's our teacher, and we take care of our own."

"Oh, Harry," Verna said with a laugh. "Adam is very kind. He always keeps his word. You have nothing to worry about."

The young people started to gather up their things, and Verna paused to talk with Blade once more. She gave her a hug and pressed the knitting materials into her hands when Blade tried to return them.

"Keep them," Verna said gently.

"Okay." Blade looked younger again, just a girl clutching her knitting. "Take care, Miss Verna." Then Blade bent down and held up a hand to Amanda Rebecca. "High five, kiddo."

Amanda Rebecca slapped her hand with a broad grin. The teenagers left the room, and Verna stood there, watching them go. Just a group of *kinner*…but the admiring look on Amanda Rebecca's face still worried him.

"I think I see it now," Adam said softly when the teens had left.

"See what?" Verna asked. She picked up a manila envelope from the desk.

"They're…just *kinner*," he said. "Different. Damaged. But *kinner*."

"Yah." Verna's chin trembled. "They are!"

"And they need you," he admitted gruffly. "I see that. You make a real difference in their lives, and they need you for support and stability, and…advice, I suppose. They look to you for something more than they get in their own lives."

Verna smiled and nodded.

"I get it," he repeated. "I might not like it. And I don't want Amanda Rebecca making friends with these young people, but I do understand, Verna."

They needed her. She needed them. She *loved* them. That wasn't going to change, was it?

Chapter Eleven

As the horse pulled the buggy down the dark road, its headlamps shining into the clear, winter evening, Verna pulled Amanda Rebecca a little bit closer. The girl sat on the seat between her and Adam, sharing a lap blanket with Verna. It was warmer that way, and the scent of her clean hair mingled with the cold, piney air outside.

"Blade won't come back?" Amanda Rebecca asked tiredly.

"No, she's done with the class now." Verna glanced at her husband, and they exchanged a solemn look. She wouldn't explain more than that.

"I like her," Amanda Rebecca said.

Adam shifted his position and rubbed a hand over his forehead.

"Me, too," Verna said quietly. "I'll miss her.

But I think she'll do well. She'll make better choices now."

"Was Blade in trouble?" Amanda Rebecca asked.

Verna looked over at Adam again, and he shrugged. "Go on and tell her, I suppose."

"*Yah*, honey, she was in trouble. She did some things that were wrong, and she got in trouble with the law. But everyone can learn from their mistakes—everyone. When we make a mistake, we don't have to keep on making it again and again. We can do better, can't we?"

Amanda Rebecca nodded.

"And I think Blade will do better."

"I don't like that name," Adam said under his breath.

Verna had nothing to say to that. It had shocked her, too, at first. Now she hardly noticed it. She cast her husband an apologetic smile. If there was one thing she'd learned from teaching that class, it was that she couldn't change anyone. She couldn't even make them into decent knitters. All she could do was love them as she found them.

Adam reined the horse in just as they turned into the drive, then he hopped out of the buggy and went back a few paces to get the mail out of the green metal mailbox. He returned a moment later with a stack of mail. He handed it over to Verna and flicked the reins again.

When they got back to the house, Verna took Amanda Rebecca and that pile of mail inside while Adam took care of the buggy. She stoked up a fire in the woodstove, and Amanda Rebecca found her kitten curled up in a little nest of blankets. With the stove burning brightly for Amanda Rebecca and Smokey, Verna went back to the pile of mail and flicked through it.

It was mostly flyers from local businesses, and there was a circle letter from Verna's side of the family. She smiled to herself—this was the first time she'd received one of these as a married woman. She opened it and looked to the last page—her *mamm* had been the last one to get the letter, and she'd forwarded it along to Verna with a stamp. She'd get to add her own good news to the letter now—telling her distant relatives about her wedding.

She'd do that later. She put it aside and looked down at the very last envelope. It was addressed to Adam Lantz, and in the return address corner of the envelope, she saw her mother-in-law's name, Amelia Lantz.

Adam's boots sounded on the step, and the door opened with a rush of cold air. He slammed the door shut behind him and put the bags of groceries on the kitchen floor.

"Adam, you got a letter from your mother," Verna said.

"Yah?" Adam took off his coat and stepped out of his boots. He rubbed his hands together to warm them.

"Amanda Rebecca, let's get you washed up for bed," Verna said, and she cast her husband a smile. "We'll work on your Bible verse, too, tonight."

Adam returned her smile, and Verna led her daughter upstairs. For the next few minutes, she helped her into her nightgown and washed her face and hands. Then Amanda Rebecca hopped up into her bed, and Verna pulled out the Bible and opened it to their verse.

"All right, honey. You repeat it after me, okay?"

"Okay."

"Children, obey your parents in the Lord: for this is right," she said.

"Children, obey…obey…"

"Your parents, in the Lord…"

And together they went over the verse. Adam had been right—this wasn't too difficult for Amanda Rebecca, after all. And after a couple of minutes going over that first verse together, Verna was pleased with the result.

"Very good," she said.

"*Yah?*" Amanda Rebecca asked.

"*Yah.* You're doing well. You'll know your Bible, and that's very important."

Amanda Rebecca snuggled down into her bed, a smile on her face.

"Good night, honey," Verna said.

"Night night."

Verna closed the door softly behind her and headed down the stairs. Adam stood by the kitchen table, the open letter in his hand. He looked up somberly as she came back into the kitchen.

"What is it?" Verna asked.

Adam pressed his lips together. "My *daet* is hurt. He fell and broke his hip."

"Oh, no!" she said. "That's terrible."

"*Yah.* And the farm is too big for my brother to handle alone. Plus, my *mamm* needs help with my father. She can't lift him. She's not strong enough, and with only Micah there to do the outdoor work, and his wife can only do so much…"

Verna's stomach sank, and she sucked in a wavering breath. She knew what was coming. She could feel it as certainly as the floorboards beneath her feet. But she didn't want to hear it.

"Mamm is asking me—us—to come back to Oregon."

Verna slid a hand over her stomach. "For how long?"

"For as long as it takes." He met her gaze uncertainly. "I know that I promised that we'd stay here in Redemption...make our home here. But my *mamm* needs help. And at my father's age, a broken hip isn't going to heal very quickly. There will be the actual healing, and then the recovery time when he gets his strength back..."

"I understand the process," she said woodenly, then swallowed hard.

"You have sympathy for what he's going through?" Adam asked, and she could see the hurt in his eyes.

"Of course, I have sympathy!" she said. "That would be horribly painful, and difficult for the family, too. I care. I really do!"

"Good." Adam's shoulders relaxed. "I'm glad to hear it, because my parents need my help."

He wanted them to leave Redemption, her home, her family, her support network...and go to Oregon where she knew no one. Her stomach knotted. "Isn't there anyone else?"

Because there was always someone! A cousin, a sister, a friend… Amish communities were full of people willing to lend a helping hand.

"Mamm asked me."

Verna didn't answer. The one reassurance she'd been given when she'd agreed to marry a stranger had been that they'd stay in Redemption. He'd *promised* her.

"She asked us, I should say," Adam amended. "Verna, look—" He reached for her hand and tugged her closer. "My relationship with my mother has been strained. I told you about that. But she needs help, and my *daet* will need someone to help him in rather intimate ways. He'll need help to the bathroom, and getting washed, and…you can't ask him to be comfortable with a cousin doing that!"

"I know!" she said, and a lump rose in her throat.

"I haven't been the best son, Verna. I need to make up for it. And I need to go help my *daet*."

She nodded. "It would be at least a year. Maybe more."

"*Yah.*" He met her gaze. "It might be that long."

"You promised me." The words stuck in her throat.

"I didn't know then that my *daet* would get hurt—"

"You *promised* me!" She met his gaze with the blaze of her own. "When we discussed this marriage, when we sat down and laid all our needs on the table between us, you told me that we'd make our home here in Redemption. That I'd have my family, my friends, my community and all the help I could possibly need all around me as I settled in to a marriage to a man I didn't know."

"You know me a little now," he said gruffly.

"A little," she agreed.

"And I haven't pushed you into anything. I respected your wishes."

Did he not understand any of this? "And I truly appreciate your kindness. But we still hardly know each other, and you want me to go to Oregon to live with your parents who I don't know, to be in a community where I know no one. I know you have to do this. I know it's the right thing to do. We must respect our parents, help them as they age, and be there for them like they were for us when we were small. But our situation is unique, Adam. Going to Oregon would be a big challenge for me."

"You'd have me, though."

"I don't please you!" she burst out. "I'm a

good *mamm* to your daughter, and that's all I do that pleases you!"

"That isn't true." He frowned.

"I have people here who need me."

"Your family would understand," he countered.

"My students need me, Adam." She raised her chin. "I make a difference for them, and I told them that my marriage wouldn't take me away from them. I gave them my word."

"Verna…" He rubbed his hands over his face.

"They are young and vulnerable, and a promise means something to them. If I break it, they won't forget. They also might never trust another Christian again. A promise matters to some people."

It mattered to her.

"Marriage takes time." Her voice shook. "It takes adjustment. You promised me that we wouldn't rush this…"

And moving away, going to his side of the family, leaving everything she'd ever known for a man she hardly knew…

"Obviously, I would never insist you do anything you don't want to." His voice grew tight. "I made that mistake in my first marriage. I…demanded too much. I won't do that with you. My parents need me in Oregon, and

I owe it to my mother to go back. You have a choice in whether you come with me or not."

Verna blinked at him. He'd leave without her? He'd simply go to Oregon with his daughter, and leave her behind?

"If you have to stay, I understand." His voice was tight, and he swallowed. "But I would like you to come."

"And what about your promise?" she asked.

"I also promised to be your husband," he said. "And you promised to be my wife. But the choice of whether or not you come with me to Oregon is yours to make."

So it didn't matter. And this man who had kissed her, but had never asked for more… This man who appreciated her mothering ways with his little girl and who was so carefully polite with her, wanted her to leave everything she knew.

"I don't know, Adam," she said.

"Don't say that," he said. "Don't say you don't know when you know full well. Will you come with me or not?"

Here in Redemption, there were young people who needed her, but who needed her in Oregon? No one. Not her in-laws—they needed Adam's help. And not Amanda Rebecca—she'd have a doting grandmother and other family members. And not Adam…

not really. Not truly. And that hadn't mattered with her community and her family all around her... Not with students who needed her to give them some guidance in their rocky lives. But faced with leaving all of this, faced with a life alone with her husband, she suddenly couldn't handle the truth of it.

They hadn't married for love. They'd married for practical reasons. Adam didn't need her. He didn't love her. And she could deal with those facts here with her friends and family surrounding her, but not out there alone.

Tears welled in Verna's eyes. "I can't do it."

Adam's heart hammered to a stop in his chest. She wouldn't come with him. His chest squeezed, and he dragged in one ragged breath. He hadn't really thought she would stay behind... Married people didn't do that. They faced life together—*lived* together.

Getting married was supposed to be the hurdle. Now that they were wed, they were... wed! They were a married couple. *Yah*, it was new, and they needed time to adjust to this, but they were well and truly married.

"You can't?" he said.

Tears shone in her eyes, and she looked away. She wiped furtively at her cheek. "You didn't marry me because you loved me. We didn't know each other. This was an arrangement based upon the fact that you needed a mother for your daughter, and I had lost all hope of ever finding a love match of my own."

She'd lost hope… How could she even think that? She was a treasure. But perhaps what she was saying was that she'd settled for less…less than love, certainly.

"But we did get married," he said.

"We did. But it wasn't because you adored me. It was practical."

"But we *are* married!" Did it have to matter how it started? They were joined before Gott! They were united and bound together for the rest of their lives. There would be no other wife for him, and no other husband for her as long as they both lived.

That fact mattered to Adam a great deal. They had taken vows before Gott and family, and they'd promised to belong to each other. He'd taken that vow very seriously—even though he'd hardly known her. He'd known what he was promising.

"Sometimes married people have different responsibilities," she said. "You can go and take care of your duties at home with your family, and I can…stay here. I can teach my class and take care of our home here."

And live separately. That was the part he was hearing between the lines.

"It would be for more than a few weeks," he said. It would be months, at the very least. It could be a couple of years.

Verna pressed her lips together, and he searched her face, looking for whatever it was she was feeling, but all he could see was sadness.

"Have I disappointed you in our short marriage so far?" he asked dismally. "Did I let you down?"

"No." She shook her head. "But we made this choice, and I thought I could handle the fact that I wasn't your love, I was just your wife. I thought I could face it if I had my community around me. But if I went away with you, I'd have to face—" Her voice caught, and she stopped.

"You'd have to face me alone?" he asked.

She straightened. "I'd have to face that we got married for practical reasons."

"We knew that…" There was no falling-in-love story. Just a practical meeting and agreement. "But that doesn't make us any less married. It doesn't make you any less my wife."

"I know. I'll still be your wife while you do what you must. And I'll be waiting for you."

Adam was doing it again—he was hoping for more from his wife, and she didn't want to give it. He wanted her to cheerfully follow him to the ends of the earth. He wanted her to trust him with her future, and to prefer being with him over anything else. He wanted her first thought to be keeping them together...

What he wanted was her love.

He hadn't earned that yet, had he? And she was right. They hadn't married for love, and he had no right to demand it of her.

"I never thought this would happen," he said quietly. "And I do mean to keep my promise to you and have us settle here in Redemption to make our home. But I have to do this—I have to help my parents. I think you'd do the same for your own."

A tear slipped down Verna's cheek, and he didn't understand her. If this hurt, why was she doing it? Why not come with him?

Except she didn't want to, and she'd rather stay here alone than venture out into Oregon with him.

Had he said too much? Had he talked too much about the things that swam around inside of him? Maybe he should have done what he'd promised himself he'd do from the start, and just kept his mouth shut! He should have said less, not more. Now she didn't trust him… Or worse, perhaps she didn't like him as well as she thought she would, now that she'd seen the real him.

Adam swallowed and looked down.

"I'll write to you regularly," he said, his throat tight. "And I'll come back as soon as I'm able."

Would they become a couple who lived in separate states? Would they be primly and properly married with no love between them? Had he stumbled into the kind of marriage that had always seemed saddest to him?

There was marriage, and there was love. And sometimes the two didn't meet. With Rebecca, he'd fought that tooth and nail. He'd refused to accept it. He'd wanted her heart, but they hadn't sorted it out. But with Verna, he wouldn't fight. It only brought out the worst in him, and he didn't want to make her cry with something he'd said.

"When will you leave?" Verna asked, her chin trembling.

"Uh—" Adam hadn't even had a chance to think that far ahead, but his parents would need help immediately. And the longer he put it off, the more it was going to hurt, and the greater the chance of he and Verna having an epic fight like the ones he'd had with Rebecca. He didn't want that.

He'd regretted those fights ever since.

"In a couple of days, I think," he said.

There was movement on the stairs, and he looked over to see his daughter standing in her nightgown, staring at them with wide eyes. She held her kitten in her arms, and the cat was looking around, blinking sleepily.

"Amanda Rebecca," he said. "You should be in bed."

The little girl's gaze flickered between them. "Are you sad?"

Verna stayed turned away, wiping at her eyes, and Adam felt his heart tug toward his wife. But how did he fix this? He wasn't even sure what had broken this early in their marriage, except that she'd gotten a good look at him by now and perhaps trusted him less.

"Let me take you back to bed," Adam said.

Adam led her back up the stairs, and she followed with Smokey in her arms. He looked over his shoulder once toward Verna, but she hadn't moved, and she didn't look back. The hallway was dark, lit only by the square of light that came up the stairs from the kitchen. He led Amanda Rebecca to her bedroom, and some moonlight spilled through her window, lighting enough of the room for her to crawl into bed. She made a little nest for her kitten beside her, and the cat began to purr.

"What's going on?" Amanda Rebecca asked.

"Your grandfather in Oregon got hurt," Adam said. "I got a letter from your *mammi* saying that she needs our help."

"Are we going to see Dawdie and Mammi?" Amanda Rebecca asked, her eyes brightening.

"*Yah*, we are," he said. "We're leaving in a couple of days. I have to sort things out first."

He had to take leave from his job, and make sure that Verna had enough money in the bank to keep paying the bills... He'd have to make sure he got a job in Oregon, too, so that he could continue to put money in the account to pay for Verna's living... Details, so many details.

And yet, his *mamm* needed his help, and the Amish community would gather round and support her, but he knew how sensitive she was. She'd think they were judging her housekeeping and her cooking. They very well might be.

"Will Mammi make me cookies?" Amanda Rebecca asked.

"*Yah*, I think she will."

"Will she like Smokey?"

"Smokey might need to stay home," he said, sinking down onto the side of her bed. He stroked the kitten's silken fur.

"I can't leave Smokey behind!" Amanda Rebecca stared up at him, stricken.

"Smokey would be with Verna." He pulled his hand away from the kitten. "Verna might need her."

Amanda Rebecca sobered. "Oh." She was silent another beat. "Oh, my." Her little chest rose and fell in quick little gasps.

"Smokey will be safe," he said quietly.

"Will I come with you, Daet?"

"*Yah*, you'll come with me."

"Will it be like before?"

"*Yah*, like before."

"And Mamm and Smokey will stay behind?" Her voice was rising in pitch, and he could almost feel her panic rising with it.

"They'll stay behind." He'd encouraged her to grow attached to Verna. He'd told her they'd be together. He'd assured her they were a family.

"Do I still have a *mamm*?" Amanda Rebecca whispered.

"Yes, you do," he said earnestly. "Verna is still your *mamm*. But we have to go help Dawdie with his hurt hip for a little while. That's all."

Or was it? Something had happened down there; something had changed between him and Verna, and he didn't know what. Would she even want him back again? Or was this the end of the tender part of their relationship—the test that proved exactly what their marriage would look like?

Would he get a letter in a month's time from Verna, asking him to stay on in Oregon, telling him that she was fine and she hoped he'd be happy out there? His imagination was running away with him, and the very thought of such a letter closed off his throat.

If only he understood women and marriage better, because he had no idea what had just happened here. But he feared that he'd just lost Verna's heart for good.

"Now go to sleep," Adam said.

"I can't sleep now, Daet. I'm too sad! I don't want to leave Smokey and Mamm."

"Not even to see Dawdie and Mammi?" he asked.

It was like her little heart was torn in two, and she started to cry. Big tears rolled down her cheeks, and she leaned toward him, her thin frame shaking with her sobs.

"Come here," he murmured, and he pulled his daughter into his arms, tucking her against his chest to keep her warm. "It's okay… It's okay…"

Except that it wasn't. He knew it, and somehow, she could feel it.

He heard the click of Verna's bedroom door shutting, and he wished he could fix all of this. But how? He had responsibilities toward his parents, old hurts to make up to his mother, and a wife who didn't trust herself to his keeping.

How naive he had been to think that marriage was his answer.

As his daughter cried, he tried to seal up all of his sadness deep inside of him. He had to be strong. He didn't have the luxury of expressing his own grief. That wasn't a privilege of a man with responsibilities. Men held it in, tamped it down and kept putting one foot ahead of the other for the ones who depended on them.

But as Amanda Rebecca's tears wound down, he couldn't help but think, *If only my wife loved me...*

If only.

Chapter Twelve

Verna lay in her bed, her heart filled with tears, and listened to Amanda Rebecca sniffling through the wall and Adam's low voice as he tried to soothe her. What had the child heard? She didn't even know, but she knew that Amanda Rebecca was deeply upset. *Kinner* always understood more than adults gave them credit for. This home, this marriage—it had all been for Amanda Rebecca. Adam wouldn't have married her, otherwise. He hadn't spotted her at a social gathering and longed to talk to her. He hadn't even chosen her first from Adel's list of available women in this community!

How foolish had she been to leap into a marriage like this one? She should have known better. But she'd been so eager for a marriage of her own, for a family and a home that would well and truly belong to her, that she'd jumped at the chance.

Eventually, it was quiet, and all Verna could think was that all of her hopes for this marriage had been dashed.

And yet…had any of her hopes even been realistic? She'd imagined living with Adam, slowly getting to know him, being surrounded by people she knew and trusted. She saw her life with Adam remaining safe and secure because of her community. She'd imagined the quilting bees she'd attend, sitting with other married women, and being able to share in those knowing looks married women cast each other when newly married women joined their ranks. She'd thought about the babies she'd have, and the *kinner* she'd raise, the meals she'd cook…all under the approving, watchful care of the women in her community. Marriage wasn't so frightening if she wasn't alone.

But that hadn't been realistic, had it?

Except, Adam had promised that they'd stay in Redemption. That had been the promise that had swayed her heart into accepting his proposal. They'd stay here.

She slept fitfully, dreaming of an empty house, of looking for Adam and not being able to find him. When she awoke, she'd overslept, and Adam had already left for work, and Amanda Rebecca stood at the foot of her bed.

"Oh!" Verna sat upright in bed. "What time is it?"

She looked at the clock next to her bed, and it was past eight already, and so their day began. Verna attempted to pretend that everything was normal, and they went downstairs to find that Adam had made oatmeal, now cold on the stove. It was a kind gesture all the same, and they heated it back up again with hot milk, fed the kitten and then got ready to head into town.

"What will we do in town?" Amanda Rebecca asked.

"I have to drop these forms off at an office for Blade," Verna said. "And then maybe we'll go get a donut at the bakery. I think you'd like that."

"Mamm?" Amanda Rebecca said softly.

"*Yah*, honey?"

"Will you come with us to see my *mammi* and *dawdie* in Oregon?"

But the thought of doing just that—going alone with a man who hadn't chosen her first, who had only chosen her for her maternal instincts... It would be harder to face the reality of his feelings for her in Oregon than it would be to face it here with her family, her community and her knitting class.

Somehow that ragtag group of knitters with their protective streak when it came to her was sadly comforting. They wanted her to be happy—and their love was almost ferocious. But it was love.

"I'm not sure I can," Verna said with forced cheer. "I have to teach my knitting class, and they depend on me. Even the courts depend on my knitting class here. I can't just leave, honey. But we'll still belong together. I'll be your *mamm*. You'll be my daughter."

But for how long? And from how far? Verna needed to think, but it was hard to do while keeping a fake smile pasted on her face, and with the scrutiny of a little girl who saw more than the adults wanted her to see.

So they finished their breakfast, and then they hitched up the buggy for the trip into town. The day was warm and the snow had melted off the pavement, leaving them a smooth ride down the narrow, winding roads that led into the town of Redemption.

But with her own heart in tatters, the ride felt longer than it usually did, and the twitter of birds enjoying the warm sunlight did nothing to soothe her soul.

Gott, what do I do?

Adam had said he'd go anyway. He'd asked her to come along and then announced that he'd be leaving in a matter of days. She could go with him, or not... And she had no idea what to do! And when she prayed, Gott wasn't answering with a warmth of His own. There was no reassurance or gentle guidance. All she felt was silence from above, and that felt like another rejection added to Adam's.

When they arrived in town, Verna dropped the documents off at the social services office on the Englisher side of town, and then she flicked the reins and headed back toward the familiar Amish streets with the bakery, the dry goods store and the quilt shop.

She parked in the back parking lot, then lifted Amanda Rebecca out of the buggy and set her on the ground.

"What kind of donut do you want?" Verna asked. "Do you want a jelly donut? Or one with cream inside?"

"I want a chocolate donut!"

Verna cast her a smile. "Then you shall have one, honey."

Verna would miss this girl and her father terribly when they were in Oregon, and maybe she could send her daughter off with some pleasant memories.

They walked together around the side of the

building, the smell of bread and yeast wafting through the air. Redemption's bakery made everyone hungry for a mile in every direction. They went in the front door, and a bell overhead tinkled to announce their arrival. There were already a few people in line—three Englishers and an old Amish man. It was the last person in line who made Amanda Rebecca gasp in delight.

"Blade!" Amanda Rebecca said.

Blade was wearing her regular black leather jacket, and she had her bag over her shoulder. She turned around and a smile split over her face.

"Hi," Blade said. "What are you doing here?"

"We're getting a donut!" Amanda Rebecca said. "What are you getting?"

"I don't know yet. I'm thinking maybe a strudel." Blade shot Verna a smile. "The Amish bakery is the best in town."

"It sure is," Verna agreed.

The line moved forward, and Verna stepped a little closer. "Blade, do you know what you'll do now? Do you have a plan yet?"

"Actually, I do have one." She licked her lips. "And I'm going to start going by Cherie now."

"Who's that?" Amanda Rebecca demanded.

"That's my legal name," she replied. "The

thing is, being called Blade was great for scaring people off, but I think I want to do things differently."

"Cherie..." Verna said softly. "It's a very nice name." She'd wanted to say it was a pretty name, but she didn't want to push it.

"Anyway, I'm going to visit my aunt in Pittsburgh. I called her up and asked if I could stay with her for a bit. I was honest. I told her that I'd been in trouble, but that I needed to start fresh."

"You just...called her?" Verna asked.

"Yep. I've been talking to this social worker—you know, trying to get some advice on starting over—and she said you have to ask for what you need. Flat out. No one's gonna guess, and if they try, they won't guess right. So I called up my aunt, told her that I'd get a job and just live straight. I said I needed help for a bit while I saved up enough for my own place. And she said okay."

"I'm so happy for you..." Verna said. "So you'll be Cherie from Pittsburgh."

"Yep. But I'm keeping the leather jacket. I like it."

Verna felt tears prick her eyes. Somehow, this girl would always be "Blade" in her heart—the tough-talking, angrily knitting sweetheart who'd shown Verna a different world. But if she was going to be going by her legal name, then Verna was proud of her. It was a step forward in the way the girl saw herself. "Cherie, you are a truly lovely girl."

"You're the only one I let talk to me like that," she replied with a wobbly smile, and then she leaned in and gave Verna a hug.

The line moved forward again, and it was Cherie's turn to order. She ordered a strudel and paid, and then Verna ordered their donuts—a chocolate donut for Amanda Rebecca and a raspberry jelly-filled donut for herself.

Cherie had to get going, since she had a shift starting soon at the burger place, and they said their goodbyes. But as she sat on the stool, nibbling at her own jelly donut, Verna's mind went back to that list Adam had written up for her.

It still rankled her a little bit to think of it, but he'd asked for what he needed, hadn't he? He'd written it down.

And now Cherie had done the same. She'd simply called up her aunt and asked for what she needed...

Somehow that seemed so backward in a marriage. She shouldn't have to say that she needed to be loved, should she? And how could a woman even ask for that? Please, love me? A man either loved a woman or he didn't.

He either couldn't see his life without her or he could. And it was a little late to decide that was of top importance.

She licked some jelly off her finger and heaved a sigh. It was very late now—the wedding was over, after all—to set up a new list of requirements for this relationship.

Still, Cherie's words hung in her mind: *You have to ask for what you need. Flat out. No one's gonna guess, and if they try, they won't guess right.*

Maybe there was wisdom in that.

"You're dripping jelly!" Amanda Rebecca laughed.

Verna caught the drip on her finger and took another bite of donut. It was something to think about, at least. She couldn't swallow. She put down the rest of her donut.

She'd miss them desperately.

For every hour that Adam worked that morning, he prayed. Something had gone wrong—terribly wrong—and he didn't know how to fix it. He had to go help his parents—there was no way around it—but Verna didn't want to come.

It was too soon, maybe. She needed more time to get to know him. They weren't even sleeping in the same bedroom yet! He'd have to go help, and if Verna didn't want to come, it wasn't unheard of for a couple to be in different places for whatever reason...for a while, at least.

Why did that hurt so much? Why did it feel like a kick to the gut to have her stay behind? Why did it feel like betrayal?

It isn't her fault, he prayed. *It isn't mine, either. I'm just being emotional about this. Help me to stop feeling this way...*

Somehow, the work was done earlier than usual that day, and the dairy manager asked if any of them wanted to head home early.

"How about you, Adam?" he asked. "You stayed late the other day. You want to head out early?"

"Uh—" Adam shrugged. "Sure. That would be nice. Thank you."

He wouldn't go home yet, though. He needed advice, and he knew enough about marriage to know that a man didn't simply go to another man and ask what he thought. If he was seeking outside advice for his marriage, then he needed a source he could trust to be honest, reliable and confidential.

There was only one person he could think of who matched that description, and it was Adel Knussli, the matchmaker who'd brought him and Verna together. Maybe she could help him to make his peace with a few months apart from Verna. He needed someone to help him get his feet back on the ground.

Adam caught a ride back with another worker who was also heading home early, and the man dropped him off at the Knussli farm that wasn't too far away. When he got out of the car, Adel poked her head out of the side door of her house.

"Adam!" she called. "Come inside. How are you?"

He exhaled a deep sigh and headed up the steps. Adel ushered him in and fixed him with a serious look.

"I'm not going to pretend I think this is a social call," she said. "What's going on?"

"Are you busy?" he asked feebly.

"My son is down for his nap, so the timing is right," she said, crossing her arms over her chest. "Now, out with it. I'll make coffee."

She turned her back and started to fill the kettle, and Adam took off his coat and hung it on a peg. Then he eased into a kitchen chair… the very one he'd sat in when he'd met Verna for the first time and looked into his wife's earnest gaze.

She'd been perfect…so what had gone wrong?

"How is Mandy doing?" Adel asked, glancing back over her shoulder.

"Amanda Rebecca," he said tiredly.

"What's that?"

"I like her to be called Amanda Rebecca."

"Oh, because she's made friends at Service Sunday, and they all called her Mandy. So I thought it was her nickname at home, too."

He sighed. "No, I want her called by her full name."

Would nothing go the way he'd asked?

Adel came back to the table, and the story tumbled out of him. How he'd been so careful to be considerate and polite. How he hoped she'd stop teaching that knitting class, but he now knew she wouldn't. He told about the accident at home in Oregon, and how his parents needed them to go back...but how he'd promised Verna they'd stay in Redemption. How he'd told her about it, how they'd argued, how they'd agreed she'd stay and he'd go...

"You'll go with your daughter, and your wife will stay behind?" Adel repeated.

"Yah."

"And you think this is a wise choice?" Adel's tone said that she thought it was dumber than a bag of rocks.

"I don't want it to be this way," he said. "I want her to come! But I promised her...and life can be complicated. How can I not help my parents when my father is injured?"

"What is holding her back?" Adel asked gently.

"She doesn't love me." The words came out in a choked rush, and he felt tears rising up inside of him.

"No, that's the story you're telling yourself," she said. "You're telling yourself a story in which your wife doesn't want to go because she doesn't care, and she has no feelings for you. That's only a story."

"Then why won't she come?" he asked. "She doesn't trust me?"

Adel was silent, and she frowned for a moment. "I know Verna rather well. And she was invested in this marriage. I know that for a fact."

"She said that she couldn't come because being alone with me would only be a reminder that our marriage was arranged," he said. "That we didn't marry for love."

"Ah." Adel nodded and her expression brightened. "There it is, then."

"There's what?" he asked helplessly.

"Adam, do you love her?"

"She's my wife."

"And you hardly know her, I know that," Adel said. "But I want you to look inside of you—at your feelings. I want you to examine how it feels to think about being separated from her for several months."

"I hate it," he said.

"Because…?"

"Because I want her with me. Because she makes everything better. She's kind, and sweet, and insightful and… Look, my first marriage was not easy. We both had expectations, and we let each other down. She wasn't happy with me! And I can't say I was overly happy with her, either. But we loved each other."

"Given time, it would have sorted out," she said.

"I don't know about that…"

"First of all, Verna is not Rebecca. She's a completely different woman. But I should also tell you that the first couple of years of marriage are a challenge for everyone," Adel said. "*Everyone*, Adam. People don't like to talk about it because it feels like failure, somehow, but it isn't failure. It's *adjustment*. And adjustment is not comfortable."

"I wanted it to be easier with Verna," he said. "We're being practical."

"Does this practical approach work?" she asked.

He didn't answer. It wasn't working out the way he'd hoped. But if he could avoid those ups and downs, the arguments and heartache, the disappointment and then the making up again... It was exhausting!

"What about your daughter?" she asked. "Does she accept Verna?"

"*Yah*, she does. She really loves her."

"Can I ask you about her full name?" Adel asked. "You are very firm about her being called her full name instead of a shortened form. Do you think that might affect your relationship with her?"

That wasn't the question he'd expected. He'd expected to have to explain why it was important to him, but suddenly he was faced with a new question.

"I hadn't thought of it," he admitted.

"Think of it now," she said. "If she wants to be called Mandy, but you will not call her by the name she likes...how does she feel?"

He thought of those big, blue, hopeful eyes, the tangle of blond hair, the way she bounced when she was excited...

"Maybe she thinks I don't understand her," he said quietly. "But I'm only trying to protect her. *Kinner* can be cruel with names. They can be bullies."

Adel nodded slowly and was silent for a few beats.

"Sometimes our best intentions give the

wrong message," Adel said gently. "Sometimes we can be right about something and still damage a relationship. You are asking my advice, *yah*?"

"Yah."

"Marriages involve hearts, Adam. You are very reserved, and you think that you're helping matters by holding back your emotions. You think you're protecting the ones you love—your daughter from being hurt by the cruelty of other children, and your wife from... what? Because I sense you are trying to protect her."

"It isn't helpful to argue over silly things just because feelings are hurt," he said. "I've learned from my earlier mistakes, and I won't do that again. It leads to misery."

"Ah. Yes, I do understand now. So, here is my advice to you. Open up. Stop holding back everything you're feeling. Tell her exactly what you're feeling—honestly, openly and kindly. But lower those defenses of yours and let it all out."

Adam stared at Adel, stunned. Had she heard anything he'd said? This was not a good idea. He knew that for a fact. He'd done this before in his previous marriage! But Adel leaned back in her chair as if satisfied.

"I'm avoiding that. It causes arguments."

"It might. You're right." She shrugged. "You two might completely lose it and finally say *exactly* what you're feeling. You're two different people from two different families with different expectations. It may very well cause some friction. It might cause a fight! But what you want—your wife's trust and commitment—won't happen without it."

"That's it?" he asked hoarsely.

"*Yah*. That's it."

He pushed his chair back. This wasn't the sort of advice he was looking for, and he wasn't sure it would be helpful. But Adel was known to be a shrewd matchmaker and a wise woman in the community. So he'd give it some thought at the very least.

"Oh, and one more thing," Adel added. "Everything in life that is worth having, is worth fighting for. That includes your marriage. If you want your wife's heart, fight for it."

Was he supposed to fight *her* for it, though? Was the community matchmaker really recommending he have a fight with his wife?

Chapter Thirteen

Verna stood at the kitchen window, looking outside at Amanda Rebecca playing in the snow. She was bundled up in two scarves and a pair of mittens—all of which Verna had made herself. The girl was rolling a snowball, and she stopped to look down at the mitts—snow was clinging to the wool and she licked at it.

Verna shook her head and chuckled. Every child ate snow off her mittens, it seemed. Verna had never seen an exception.

"You'll miss them."

Verna turned back to her father, who sat at the kitchen table, Smokey nestled in his arms. The kitten seemed to love her father—curled up in a little purring ball of fluff on his broad chest. He'd come by to see her, and Verna had nearly burst into tears at the sight of him. It was Marvin who'd bustled Amanda Rebecca outside to play, and Verna had spilled the story out to him.

"I will miss them," she said.

"Verna, you know you should be going with him to Oregon," her father said.

Verna was silent for a moment. "He'll come back."

"He's your husband."

"I know."

Of anyone, she *knew*! This was her husband until death parted them, and somehow she'd imagined those vows clicking everything into place. It hadn't worked that way.

"Relationships are fragile things, Verna. They don't stay the same. They either grow, or they shrink. One or the other. And if he leaves without you, your marriage *will* change. He won't come back the same man."

Verna sank into the chair opposite her father, and she looked at his familiar, lined face, his grizzled beard and his kind eyes. She'd heard the stories about their courtship and marriage over and over again in her youth. How Daet had asked Mamm home from singing, and how she'd been sad because their dog had run away, and Daet brought her a puppy the very next weekend. It was sweet, and perfect. And her parents had never been anything but happy.

That was what she'd given up hope of ever finding for herself.

"Daet, you married Mamm because you loved her," she said, tears welling up in her eyes.

"Has Adam been mean to you?" Her father leaned forward, those kind eyes suddenly sparking with protectiveness. Smokey looked up and gave a little mew of alarm. He settled a warm hand on top of the kitten, and Smokey settled back against his chest.

"No, Daet. He's kind. He's polite. He's… careful."

"Good." He leaned back.

Was it good, though? She rubbed her hands over her face. "I'm afraid to leave here. I don't want to go to some community where I don't know anyone—to some mother-in-law who will never see me as good enough for her son, I'm sure."

"You don't know that, Verna."

"He promised me we'd stay here, Daet! He said we'd stay here, and I'd have you and Mamm, and the rest of the family, and my friends, and…it would be easier."

"For the sound advice and the friendly support," her father said.

"*Yah*! Exactly. When you have to leave everyone you love behind—"

"Except for your husband."

She nodded. "Except for him… Daet, I don't think I can do this alone. I really don't! I don't want to be a lonely wife crying behind the outhouse at Service Sunday. If we'd married for love I'd have him to lean on. But he doesn't love me. I married a man I hardly knew! And…he's breaking a promise already."

And she'd started to feel all sorts of sweet, tender, overwhelming emotions for him. She cared about his feelings, and his thoughts. She longed for more of his kisses. And when he said he'd leave without her, her heart had torn in two. Because…

It hit her square in the chest. Because she loved him. Such a short time together, and she loved her husband.

Her father nodded slowly, his thoughtful gaze locked on her face. "What would you need to go along with him?"

"What?"

"What would it take to make you feel secure enough with Adam for you to go to Oregon?"

"I don't know…"

Because Verna loved him, and he was willing to leave without her. That meant he didn't feel what she was feeling, and she'd be traveling to stay with his family with no guarantee of ever coming back, and she'd be hoping for tenderness and love and very likely wouldn't get it. But if they stayed here in Redemption, she might not have his love, but she'd have her community, and her family, and a place *here*.

"I'm going to let you in on a little marriage secret," her father said. "It's called making a deal."

"A deal?"

"He wants to go to Oregon to help his parents. It's noble and good. What do you need to make it worth the trip for you?"

"It's not about the trip—"

"I know, I know," he said. "It's about being scared, and not knowing if you can face your marriage all by yourself out there."

She nodded.

"Okay, so what would make it so that you could go with him? What do you need? Sometimes in a marriage, you need to strike a deal."

"I thought marriage was about love and selflessness. You're supposed to sacrifice—"

"It is, it is, but it's also the union of two people who mean well, but who think differently," her father said. "This is the practical side of things. Marriage is also about communication, and letting the other person understand your feelings and what you need. Your *mamm* wouldn't be half so happy with me if she didn't tell me straight what she needed from me. If she needs me to help out in the house more, or if she needs me to listen to her talk about her troubles, or if she needs me to give her more compliments. I'd never figure it out on my own! She *tells me*, Verna. It's behind closed doors, but she does tell me."

Verna hadn't realized that. She'd always thought her parents were in tune with each other, walking in lockstep. They were united, and very much in love with each other. But their private conversations never happened where anyone else could overhear.

"It's not so romantic, is it?" she asked.

"Romance?" Her father barked out a laugh. "Romance is forty years of marriage! It's coming home to each other, and doing chores together, and raising *kinner*. It's about sitting down with the wife who just had your fifth child, and telling her that she's just as beautiful now as she ever was, even though her emotions are on a wild ride and her body is still recovering. It's about choosing each other day after day. Romance is when your wife puts your plate down in front of you, and she's made sure you have the chicken leg because she knows you like it. And romance is also two people putting their needs on the table between them, and figuring out a deal that lets them both get what they need. That's romance, dear girl. Romance rolls up its sleeves and gets dirty."

"I didn't realize that..."

Dealmaking... It sounded too practical, almost like that list Adam had written out for her on the day of their wedding, giving her his expectations with his daughter.

"*Yah*, we want a story that sounds good to tell the *kinner*," her father said. "But you only get stories to tell the *kinner* by taking a risk and choosing your husband. So I'd suggest you sit down with Adam, and you decide what you need to make that trip to Oregon. There's something. You'll figure it out."

But what did she need? What would give her the confidence she'd need to take that long trek with him out to Oregon and face all those unknowns? What did she need most?

Outside, she heard the clop of hooves and the rattle of a buggy.

"Daet!" Amanda Rebecca shouted from outside. "Hi, Daet!"

Verna's father rose to his feet and handed the kitten over to Verna. She smoothed a hand over Smokey's downy back. Her father picked up his felt hat and dropped it onto his head.

"That's my cue to leave," he said with a tender smile. "Talk to your husband, Verna. I believe he's a good man, and he means well. But you're going to have to be strong enough to hold your own. And I'm sure you can."

Verna followed her father to the door. He put on his boots and coat, and with one last smile, he headed outside. She stood in the doorway, Smokey held close in her arms, watching him as he trudged across the snow toward Adam's returning buggy.

"Hello!" her father called out. "Nice to see you home from work early. I just stopped in to have a coffee with my daughter."

Adam hopped down from the buggy and shook her father's hand. Their voices lowered, but they both smiled, then her father headed over to his own buggy. A brisk wind whipped her dress around her legs from where she stood in the open doorway, and she shivered.

Verna shut the door quietly and leaned against the door frame, her heart hammering in her throat. What did she need from Adam? The one thing she wanted couldn't be demanded. She wanted him to love her.

She headed over to the desk in the sitting room. Her list was short, but she knew what she needed now.

* * *

Adam watched as his father-in-law's buggy headed up the drive.

"Daet? Daet?" Amanda Rebecca said. "Do you want to build a snowman with me?"

His daughter looked up at him with bright eyes. Her cheeks were cold reddened, but she was bundled up in scarves that he recognized as his wife's handiwork. If knitting could show how well a child was loved, Amanda Rebecca was swathed in it.

"Amanda Rebecca..." He looked down at her thoughtfully. "Do your friends call you Mandy?"

The girl froze, her expression hesitant. She was afraid of getting into trouble, he could tell.

"It's okay if they do," he said.

"Is it?" she asked.

He nodded.

"Okay. Then they do. And I like it. I like being Mandy."

"Do you want...do you want me to try to call you Mandy sometimes, too?" he asked.

Amanda Rebecca's eyes lit up. "Oh, Daet, I would love it!"

Tears misted his eyes. He'd come so very close to missing this opportunity to make her light up like that.

"I won't call you Mandy all the time," he said gently. "But I will sometimes, okay?"

His daughter nodded with eyes bright. It would be a step forward, and maybe his daughter would relax a little more with him. Maybe he could stop trying to fight battles that hadn't even come yet and pray for more wisdom instead.

"I'm going to go inside and talk to Mamm for a bit," Adam said. "You play outside a little longer, okay?"

Amanda Rebecca didn't need to be told twice. She loved playing in the snow. She marched off through some deep, untouched snow, then squatted down, her tongue outstretched, trying to reach it.

He headed up the steps, then stomped the extra snow off his boots before he opened the door and headed inside. Verna stood by the stove, the kitten in her arms, and he cast her a hesitant smile.

"Hi." He pulled off his coat and hung it up. "I got off early today."

"That's nice they let you come home."

"I told Amanda Rebecca that we can call her Mandy," he said.

"You did?" A smile split his wife's face. "Adam, she will really love that."

"Yah..." He'd seen it already. He had some

learning to do when it came to the women in his home, didn't he? "I don't want to tell you a lie about where I've been, though. I went to see Adel first. I wanted some advice."

Verna's smile evaporated and her face paled. "Oh? And what did she say?"

"She said—" He cleared his throat. "She said I should relax about Amanda Rebecca's nickname." He smiled faintly. "And she said I need to open up to you and say what's on my mind. She said I have to stop being so reserved. It's not helping—according to her."

"And what's on your mind?" Verna asked.

Not like this. Not some tense standoff between a husband and wife. He put his boots on the mat and then crossed the kitchen. He bent down and pecked her lips gently.

"This is hard for me," he said. "But I'm just going to say it. I want you to come with me to Oregon."

"I know." She nodded.

"And I... I know this is quick because we've only known each other a matter of weeks, but Verna, you are my wife. And when I married you, I prayed we'd love each other. So while I know you don't love me yet, the fact of the matter is, Gott answered my prayer. And I fell in love with you." Verna blinked up at him, but he plunged on. "And that's why the thought of you not coming with me to Oregon hurts something fierce. I don't want to go without you. And I want to be the man you lean on, and the man you depend on. And I figure I need to earn that right. So here's the thing. I'm not going if you don't come with me. That's that. I just won't go. Either we go together or not at all, because I love you, and I'd miss you too much."

Adam searched around inside himself, looking for anything else that needed saying, but that summed it up pretty well. Tears misted Verna's eyes.

"Do you mean it?" she whispered.

"*Yah*, I do." He paused, feeling like he was probably missing out on something here, some female way of seeing things. "Which part?"

"All of it. That you…love me."

"*Yah*. I hope that one day, you might—"

"I do love you!" She stepped a little closer. "That's why it hurt so much that you'd go without me."

His heart stammered in his chest. Somehow, when he thought about how this would go, he hadn't considered this option—the one he wanted most. "You do?"

Verna nodded. "*Yah*. I do."

His heart suddenly flooded full and overflowed, and he lowered his lips over hers.

He pulled her close into his arms, and then she started to laugh. He looked down to see that she was trying to protect the kitten from being squeezed.

"I love you…" he breathed. "I really do. And if you love me…"

He didn't even know how to finish that, but he knew that it meant everything. It meant that all of his prayers had been answered in three little words.

"You gave me a list of your expectations when we got married," she said, pulling back out of his arms.

He winced. "I'm sorry about that—"

"No, it's okay," she said, and she pulled a slip of paper out of her apron. "I have a list of my own."

He swallowed. "Oh?"

"It's what I need to go to Oregon with you."

He accepted the slip of folded paper from her fingers and opened it. There were only a few words written there in neat, fluid handwriting.

I need your whole heart.

Tears blurred his vision, and he swallowed against the lump in his throat. He lowered the page, slipped a hand behind her neck and pulled her into another kiss. When he pulled back, he nodded.

"Done."

"*Yah?*"

"You have it. You always will. Now, we have to decide together—do we go to Oregon and help my parents, or not?"

"We go," she whispered.

"*Danke*. I truly mean it. We'll come back to Redemption as fast as we can. I promise you that."

"Okay." She nodded. "But I really think we need to bring Smokey with us. Amanda Rebecca will be heartbroken otherwise."

And she was right, of course. He knew his daughter would be beside herself with worry if they left the cat behind. There had to be a way to bring Smokey along.

Adam nodded. "Whatever you think is best, Mamm."

Verna laughed softly. "I do like the sound of that."

"And if I could ask just one more thing?" Adam said hopefully. This was delicate, but he did want to fall asleep next to his wife so very badly… "We have three bedrooms in this house…" He paused, wondering how he could say this out loud. "And when we go to Oregon, there will be even fewer. I suggest that until we leave, we… share a bedroom."

Color touched her cheeks. "*Yah*, Adam. I think that would be best, too."

That covered every single hope and longing Adam had in his heart. Every last one. All he could do was send up a prayer of thanksgiving.

Epilogue

Six months later, when the sun shone warm on a June afternoon, Verna arrived at Delia's flower farm for a visit. She'd come alone today, since Mandy was visiting with Verna's parents, and Adam had headed back to his job at the dairy. Gott had answered prayers, and they'd hired him back again.

The flower farm was exquisite this time of year—rows upon rows of blooms in the sunny gardens, bright colors against dark loam. The scent of flowers wafted over to her, and bees buzzed close by. She'd missed this old place—her friend, her community, her family. She'd missed them with every beat of her heart when they were away, but the trip had been a good one, too.

Delia came running out of a greenhouse, her skirt held up to let her legs move freely, and she laughed and hugged Verna as soon as Verna's feet were on the ground.

"I didn't know you were back!" Delia said. "You look wonderful, Verna. I can't put my finger on it, but you look radiant."

"Oh, you've just missed me, that's all," Verna said with a laugh. "We got back to Redemption a couple of days ago."

"Well, come inside and tell me all about Oregon," Delia said. "I've got some muffins made—not much else, I'm afraid. The boys power through everything I cook."

"As they should," Verna said and allowed her friend to lead the way up into her kitchen.

"Where are the boys?" Verna asked.

"They're fishing with an uncle today," she said. "I gave them the day off. They've been working so hard. But what about you? How was Oregon?"

Verna sank into a kitchen chair and accepted a glass of water. "It was actually wonderful. Adam's mother was born an Englisher, and so she could really understand what I was doing with my knitting class. I don't think anyone else could have! And she was really kind and grateful for our help. I got to know Adam's family and hear stories about him from when he was growing up, and..."

Her mind went back to the conversation-filled days, to his old father who was in considerable pain, but was still kind to her. She remembered tucking Mandy into a little trundle bed in her cousins' bedroom, and then going to bed in the little bedroom next door with Adam…just like they'd been doing this forever.

"…and?" Delia probed.

"It was just very nice. I was so afraid of going there alone with Adam, but really, it helped us to feel more like a married couple. I don't know how to explain it."

"You don't have to," Delia said. "I get it."

Verna took a carrot muffin from a plate and peeled off the paper. She was hungry— but she always seemed to be hungry lately. Delia cocked her head to one side, looking at her thoughtfully.

"Verna, either you've gained some happiness weight, or…" Delia winced. "I'm going to say it. Verna, are you expecting?"

Verna felt her face heat and she nodded. "I'm not going to deny a little happiness weight. Adam keeps gobbling up everything I bake, and so I eat it right along with him. My mother-in-law called it the Marriage Ten. For me, though, it might end up being the Marriage Twenty!"

"You look wonderful," Delia said. "It's a blessing!"

"Also… I'll let you in on the secret," Verna said. "I'm four months along. I didn't think anyone could tell yet."

"Well, I couldn't tell, exactly. I more guessed," Delia said. "But how wonderful! Verna, I'm so happy for you!"

"*Yah, danke*, I couldn't be happier…or hungrier." Verna laughed at her own little joke and took another bite of muffin. "But it's a secret still, Delia! Only my parents know. I wrote them as soon as I found out. But we aren't telling anyone else yet."

"Does Amanda Rebecca know?" Delia asked.

"*Yah*, it was hard to keep the secret from her. She doesn't miss a thing."

"I wouldn't count on keeping that secret for much longer then!" Delia laughed. "*Kinner* talk!"

And Delia was probably right. Besides, her pregnancy would become too pronounced to hide behind a loose apron soon enough, and the women in Redemption would help her to celebrate her new baby. They'd come with advice and natural remedies for things like morning sickness and fatigue. They'd bring baby clothes and help her to fill the bottom of her hope chest with everything she might need.

That's what community was about.

"I'm glad you're home again," Delia said with a warm smile.

As Verna ate her muffin and chatted with her friend, she let her gaze wander out the window to the sunlight playing over rows upon rows of flowers, and she sent a prayer of thanksgiving Heavenward.

She was thankful for her husband, her daughter and this little baby inside of her whom she loved with all her heart already. She was thankful for friendships, and family, and in-laws in Oregon who'd accepted her right away, and for all the blessings Gott had poured out for her that she'd almost been too afraid to gather up.

But the greatest blessing of all was Adam, the man she couldn't wait to see again tonight when he got home from work. She'd have food on the table, and he'd kiss her as he always did now, and he'd tell her two new baby name ideas, she was sure. He seemed to be overflowing with them!

"What about your knitting class?" Delia asked. "I think they have the Froese sisters teaching it now, don't they? Will you take it back?"

"I don't think I'll be able to," Verna said. "Not with a new baby and Mandy. I think my days of knitting classes are over for now."

"Will you miss it?" Delia asked.

Verna nodded. She would. She'd miss the teens she'd gotten to know, and the glimpse into their world that they allowed when they finally trusted her enough. The rest of her class—Tia, Harry and Abigail—had all moved on from the knitting class, too, and Verna's heart went out to them, wherever their lives took them. She'd likely not see them again, but she hoped they always carried her advice with them, that if they found themselves in need of support, or love, or encouragement, that they'd seek out the nearest church.

"But there's a season for everything," Verna said, resting her hand on the soft swell of her abdomen, "and that season will roll around again, I'm sure. Until then, I'm just thankful for the family Gott gave me. I didn't think I'd have a family of my own, Delia, and I feel like Gott opened up the windows of Heaven and poured out so much blessing on me that I hardly have room for it all."

And she meant that from the bottom of her heart.

* * * * *

*If you enjoyed this book by Patricia Johns,
pick up these previous titles in her
Amish Country Matches miniseries:*

The Amish Matchmaking Dilemma
Their Amish Secret
The Amish Marriage Arrangement

Available now from Love Inspired!

Dear Reader,

I hope you are enjoying these stories about the women of Redemption and their stalwart matchmaker. If you'd like to see more of my books, come find me online at patriciajohns.com where I have quite a backlist of Amish and sweet romance stories.

If you enjoyed this book, I hope you'll consider posting a review. It helps other readers to find my stories, and I truly appreciate every review my readers take the time to post.

You can also find me on Facebook, Instagram and Twitter where I enjoy connecting with my readers. If you came by and said hello, you'd make my day!

Patricia